...esent

...ure!

A... ...ost popular

r... ...orgettable

...w."

KEIR DULLEA · SUSAN PENHALIGON

Leopard in the Snow

Guest Stars

KENNETH MORE · BILLIE WHITELAW

featuring GORDON THOMSON as MICHAEL

and JEREMY KEMP as BOLT

Produced by JOHN QUESTED and CHRIS HARROP
Screenplay by ANNE MATHER and JILL HYEM
Directed by GERRY O'HARA

An Anglo-Canadian Co-Production

**ON RELEASE DURING 1978
IN UNITED KINGDOM, REP. OF IRELAND,
AUSTRALIA AND NEW ZEALAND**

Books you will enjoy
by SARA CRAVEN

TEMPLE OF THE MOON

Gabrielle had gone to Yucatan in Central America in a last attempt to salvage her marriage-that-wasn't-a-marriage to James Warner—and immediately found herself in conflict with the disturbing Shaun Lennox. And it would be no help to any of them if she should be so foolish as to fall in love with Shaun . . .

WILD MELODY

On the strength of her brief holiday romance with Jeremy Lord, Catriona left her quiet Scottish home and came up to London to marry him. But Jeremy, of course, had forgotten all about her by now—and instead she found herself involved with his sophisticated uncle Jason. Who was even more out of her league than Jeremy had been . . .

A GIFT FOR A LION

When Joanna landed herself uninvited on the tiny, mysterious Mediterranean island of Saracina she promptly fell into the hands of its stern overlord, Leo Vargas—which probably served her right. But the real danger facing her was not to her person but to her heart!

STRANGE ADVENTURE

Young Lacey Vernon was being more or less forced to marry the Greek tycoon Troy Andreakis to save her father from ruin—but as time went on she began to realise, unwillingly, that perhaps she wasn't dreading him as much as she had imagined she was. But that was before she learned what kind of a man Troy really was . . .

A PLACE OF STORMS

by

SARA CRAVEN

MILLS & BOON LIMITED
17–19 FOLEY STREET
LONDON W1A 1DR

First published 1977
Philippine copyright 1978
This edition 1978

ISBN 0 263 72564 2

Set in Linotype Plantin 10 on 10½ pt.

Made and printed in Great Britain by
Richard Clay (The Chaucer Press), Ltd., Bungay, Suffolk

CHAPTER ONE

'ANDY—please! You've just got to help me. There's no one else I can turn to.'

From her seat on the Persian rug in front of the fire, Andrea Weston thought wryly that Clare's flair for the dramatic was going to be wasted on anything so mundane as marriage. But this time—this time she was going to turn a deaf ear to it, and to that deliberate use of the diminutive of her name. She had heard it all before when Clare wanted to be rescued from some childhood or schooldays scrape of her own making.

'No one?' she asked caustically, letting her eyes rest on the magnificent sapphire and diamond ring adorning Clare's left hand.

Clare noticed the direction of her gaze and shuddered.

'Peter mustn't know.' She sounded genuinely panic-stricken. 'Promise me you won't tell him.'

'Oh, I can safely promise that.' Andrea pushed back her long fall of chestnut hair. 'How can I tell him what I don't know myself?' She saw Clare open her mouth and hastily forestalled her. 'And I don't want to know either, Clare. We're not children any longer. I may have been able to talk you out of trouble with Nanny and Sister Benedict, but you're a big girl now. You've got to learn to solve your own problems.'

'Oh, Andy!' Clare's shoulders drooped forlornly. 'Don't be hard on me.'

'It's time someone was,' Andrea told her honestly. 'Uncle Max has spoiled you rotten for years, and you know it.'

Clare nodded humbly, her enormous blue eyes filled with tears. 'I do know—but you've got to help me, Andy. You're my last hope.'

'Nonsense!' Andrea hoped her voice was sufficiently robust. 'Whatever you've done, my advice is go to Peter and make a clean breast of it. You're going to be married to him in six weeks and you can't hope to hide things from him then ...' Her voice trailed away uneasily as Clare buried her face in her hands and began to cry in real earnest.

'Oh, love!' Andrea got up and went to sit on the big white chesterfield next to Clare, putting a comforting arm round her cousin's heaving shoulders. 'It can't be as bad as all that, surely.'

'But it can.' Clare's voice was choked with sobs. 'I'm in such a mess—and there may not be any wedding, and I'll make Daddy ill again, I know it.'

Andrea sighed. 'Then you'd better tell me,' she said wearily. An awful thought occurred to her. She stared at her cousin. 'Clare—you haven't ... I mean, you aren't ...'

'Oh, no.' Clare shook her head vigorously. In spite of her distress a faintly dreamy look crossed her lovely features. 'Anyway, Peter has always said he has far too much respect for me to try and anticipate our marriage vows.'

'How—how honourable of him,' Andrea said a little wildly. Her own private view of Clare's fiancé was that he was a stuffed shirt, and Clare's artless disclosure seemed to confirm this. Clare was an entrancingly beautiful girl with her shining cap of blonde hair, and a figure just verging towards the voluptuous, and Andrea could not imagine any red-blooded man being able to resist at least an attempt to make love to her. However, Clare seemed convinced that he was the only man who could make her happy and Andrea supposed that this was really all that mattered. Her own doubts about whether Peter would ever have proposed to Clare if she had not been Maxwell Weston's daughter she kept strictly to herself.

'All right,' she said gently. 'Then what is wrong?'

Clare gave a long sigh that seemed to come up from her toes. 'There's—there's someone else,' she said.

'Another man?' Andrea could hardly believe it. Admittedly Clare had played the field before she met Peter. Since her early teens there had hardly been a time when she was not madly in love with someone, either in the ecstatic throes of first meetings, or the tears and recriminations of parting. Yet Andrea would have been ready to swear that her devotion to Peter had been utterly single-minded. 'Do I know him?'

Clare shook her head. 'He's—French.'

'I suppose you met him when you were staying with Martine in Paris.' Andrea racked her brains to remember some of the details of Clare's scanty letters. 'Surely it can't be that appalling Jacques! Oh, Clare ...'

'No, no,' Clare assured her hastily. 'Though it is all his fault indirectly,' she added, her eyes kindling with resentment. 'If I hadn't been so absolutely devastated about him, I'd never have contemplated getting involved with the Levallier man.'

'So his name's Levallier,' Andrea persevered. 'How did you meet him?'

'I didn't.' Clare gave her a limpid look.

Andrea closed her eyes and prayed for patience. 'You can't possibly be in love with someone you've never met—not even you ...'

'But I'm not in love with him. I tell you I've never set eyes on him. It was just ... oh, when Jacques threw me over like that for that awful Janine, I just wanted to die. I've never felt so wretched before. Nothing seemed to matter any more, so when he wrote and suggested we should get married, it seemed a godsend—an absolute face-saver.'

Andrea stared at her, slim arched brows raised incredulously. 'A complete stranger wrote to you and proposed?'

'Not exactly. I—I had been writing to him before that. He's a cousin of Martine's—second or third, from what she said, but her family don't talk about him much. He's some kind of black sheep, apparently. I think he must have been living abroad somewhere, but he's come back because he's inherited this chateau in Auvergne, and he wrote to Martine's parents, extending an olive branch, I think. They were highly indignant about this,' Clare added reflectively.

'Martine and I thought it was a shame, and so we decided if they didn't want to reply to his letter, we would. We sent a joint letter, as a joke really.'

'And he replied?'

'Oh yes. It was rather a nice letter—amused, as if he guessed what we were up to. But Martine wouldn't write again. She was afraid her parents would find out and cancel the winter sports holiday they were planning, so I wrote the next letter myself. Eventually we had quite a correspondence going. I told him all kinds of things. I even told him about Jacques when it was all over. It was marvellous to be able to pour it all out to someone who wasn't actually involved, or who knew either of us. And that was when he proposed.'

'But why? Did he give a reason, or was he just sorry for you?'

'No. He made that very clear. In fact,' Clare said rather coldly. 'He implied I'd asked for it. No, the proposal was purely a business proposition. He stressed that. He needed a wife urgently to settle some legal difficulty—he didn't really specify what—and as I was so miserable and at a loss, he thought we could help each other.'

'But surely you ended it there—when you saw what deep waters you were getting into?'

Clare did not meet her cousin's clear hazel eyes. 'I—accepted,' she said after a pause.

'Clare!'

'Oh, don't look at me like that. I told you—I was so desperate about Jacques, I'd have done anything. I'd have married Bluebeard if he'd asked me. And this was a way out. If I was engaged to this Blaise Levallier, then Jacques would see I didn't care. Which I didn't, of course,' she added wonderingly. 'I wish I'd realised it earlier.'

Andrea groaned. 'So do I,' she said with feeling. 'You must have been out of your mind!'

Clare considered. 'I felt very calm, actually. After what I'd just been through with Jacques, a *mariage de convenance* sounded like bliss, I don't mind telling you. I meant to go through with it, too. He sent me some things to sign—and some money—to buy my trousseau with, I suppose. I hadn't told him about Daddy, and he probably thought I was living *au pair* with Martine's family.'

'Probably.' Andrea looked at her in consternation. 'What did you do with the money?'

'I didn't spend it,' Clare assured her. 'I might have done, I admit, but then Daddy had his first heart attack. When Mummy sent for me, I forgot about everything else.'

She got up and walked across the room to the small Regency bureau against one wall. 'The money's all here—every franc. You can count it if you like.'

'No, thanks.' Andrea put out a restraining arm and caught her cousin's skirt. 'Never mind the money. Just tell me the rest. There is more, I presume.'

'Yes.' Clare returned to the chesterfield and sat down. 'But you know it really. I met Peter—I think we both knew at once there would never be anyone else—and Blaise went out of my head altogether. When I did think about it, it just seemed like a bad dream.'

'I can imagine,' Andrea said drily. 'And when did you wake up?'

Clare reached for her cream leather handbag. 'When these came.' She drew a small packet of letters secured by a rubber band out of the bag. 'Martine sent the first one on.' She sent Andrea a stricken look. 'It was full of details about the arrangements for the wedding. I was petrified. I—I didn't answer. I hoped he might think the letter hadn't arrived and just—give up.'

'But he didn't.'

'No,' Clare admitted despondently. 'He wrote again, and this letter came straight here, so he must have had me traced in some way. He sent me the money for my air fare and said that if I let him know when I'd be arriving, he would hire a car to meet me at the airport, and I could drive out to St Jean des Roches—that's where his chateau is. I—I had to reply, so I said I was ill,' Clare concluded in the tone of one blessed with divine inspiration. 'A few weeks went by and I heard nothing more, so I began to hope that he'd given me up as a bad job. Peter and I were engaged by now, and everything was sheer heaven. Then another letter arrived. It was totally different from the others—really hateful. He said he was sure I must have recovered by now and that the wedding had to take place almost at once.' She sighed and bent her head. 'I—I couldn't very well ignore that, so I wrote to him and told him I'd changed my mind ...'

'You didn't tell him about Peter?'

'No, and I'm glad I didn't.' Clare's pretty face became stormy. 'Because this arrived back—by return of post, I should think.' She extracted one of the letters from the bundle on her lap and handed it to Andrea.

'Mademoiselle,' it began unpromisingly, 'Much as I may regret your sudden reluctance to proceed with our agreed contract, I have to tell you that my own plans are now too far advanced to permit any withdrawal on your part. Unless you present yourself here in accordance with our agreement, I shall take action against you for breach of promise. I have, you may remember, your written consent to the marriage.'

The letter was typewritten, but the signature was there, black and bold and uncompromising, the downstrokes with the pen thick and formidable as if they had been made by an angry man.

Andrea's lips were compressed as she refolded the single thin sheet.

'I think he means it,' she said, meeting her cousin's anxious look. 'Can you still sue people for breach of promise?'

Clare shuddered. 'I don't know, but even if he can't, there's bound to be the most awful scandal. The newspapers have been looking for something involving Daddy for ages. I—I just can't do it to him, Andy. He could have another attack—and this time it could be fatal. The specialist warned us ...' She began to cry again and Andrea looked at her with compassion.

'Don't worry, love.' She gave Clare a quick hug. 'It won't happen. We won't let it.'

'We?' Clare caught her breath on a little sob. 'You mean you will help me?'

Andrea was taken aback for a moment. 'Well, I'll do anything I can,' she said cautiously. 'Only it's difficult to see what ...'

'The first thing is to get that letter back—the one where I said I'd marry him.' Clare sat up eagerly, miraculously restored to optimism. 'And that contract thing. I must have been mad!'

'Yes,' Andrea agreed drily. 'What are you going to do? Write and ask him for them so that you can check if they're legally binding? I don't think he'll swallow that somehow.'

'No, of course he wouldn't. You'll have to go to St Jean des Roches and steal them back. He's bound to keep them at the chateau.'

'*I'll* have to go ...' Words momentarily failed Andrea, then she looked squarely at her cousin. 'No, Clare.'

'But it's the obvious solution. I daren't go myself. He might force me to do—anything.'

'And what will he do when I arrive—get out the welcome mat, I suppose.' Andrea gave her an irritated look.

'Well, he would—if he thought you were me,' Clare said.

'Now I know you're mad,' Andrea said faintly. 'You really think I'm going to career halfway across France and pretend to be you in order to steal some letters from a man whom by your own admission you've led up the garden path. You say yourself you dare not go anywhere near him. If he thinks I'm you, he might force me into—anything!'

'No, no.' Clare spoke soothingly. 'If anything like that were to happen, you would simply tell him who you were. He has no hold over you, after all.'

Andrea stared at her wonderingly. 'You've got it all worked out, haven't you?' she managed at last.

'I've had precious little else to think about,' Clare said tartly. 'I couldn't possibly go. I've got the wedding to get ready for, for one thing, and Peter would think it very odd if I dropped all the preparations and disappeared to France. And I can't delay much longer, or this Levallier man will come to London and then everyone will know.' She shivered and turned pleading eyes on Andrea. 'Peter would be so angry. He might leave me. And his beast of a mother would encourage him—she's always hated me. Oh, Andy, if I lose Peter, I don't know what I'll do. I shan't want to go on living.'

Andrea looked at her coldly. 'You could always marry this—Levallier. It can't have seemed such a repulsive prospect at one time.'

'You're utterly heartless.' Clare's lips were trembling ominously again. 'And I thought you would understand.'

'I do understand—I think.' Andrea gave an exasperated sigh. 'But it's not as simple as you seem to think. You're asking me to commit an actual crime—to steal some letters.'

'But they're my letters.' Clare looked at her wide-eyed.

'I think the law takes a different view,' Andrea said grimly.

'Oh—the law.' Clare dismissed the combined weight of French and British justice with a wave of her hand. 'I wrote that letter, and I want it back. And you're the ideal person to get it for me!'

'How have you arrived at that conclusion? Is there some criminal element in the family that I don't know about?'

'No, but you do work in public relations, so you're used to dealing with awkward people. And you are owed some leave—I heard you telling Mummy so last week.' She paused, her eyes searching her cousin's unyielding face. 'Andy, if you won't do it for me, do it for Daddy. He's always treated you as if you were his own daughter . . .'

'If you're reminding me that he paid for my school fees as well as yours, it's unnecessary.' The colour was suddenly heightened in Andrea's cheeks. 'Blackmail must be catching, I think.' She stood up abruptly and reached for her suede coat and bag.

'Now I've made you angry,' Clare said disconsolately. 'I didn't mean it, Andy. I'm just so worried.'

'I know.' Andrea relented slightly as she studied the woebegone figure. 'All I can promise is that I'll think about it. There must be some solution.'

'Oh, there is,' Clare said flatly. 'I can write and tell him to go to hell.' She gave a little shudder. 'Oh, Andy, there'd be the most dreadful row. If there was a court case, it would be in all the papers. It would destroy Mummy and Daddy. They've worked so hard to keep our private lives —private.' Her eyes widened as another dreadful thought occurred to her. 'They might even find out about Jacques and drag him into it.'

Andrea's thoughts were troubled as she descended the staircase to the hall. Although she had resented Clare's words, they had struck home, she was forced to acknowledge. Her own parents were dead, her father when she was a small child, her mother more recently. But this large London house had been a second home to her for as long as she could remember. Without a hint of patronage, neither Uncle Max nor Aunt Marian had ever allowed her to want for anything. Nor had she felt any sense of obligation—until now.

She reached the bottom of the stairs and stood for a moment, rummaging in her bag for her car keys. Whatever happened, it was essential that the news of Clare's folly should be kept from her uncle, she thought. She had been in London when he had suffered that first attack, and had stayed with her aunt, and she knew better than Clare just how precarious his health was, and how entirely necessary it was that he should have a considerable period without stress or worry.

She gave a little restless sigh, and stood turning the keys in her hands, her eyes fixed unseeingly on the parquet floor. If Peter had been a different sort of man, she thought she might have gone to him and pleaded for Clare. But as things were, she knew Clare was right to keep it from him. His conventional soul would be shocked to its core, and he would possibly decide that all his mother's none too subtle hints about Clare's unsuitability as a wife were well founded. In all justice, Andrea supposed that Lady Craigie had right on her side. Clare's sowing of her wild oats had been pretty blatant at times, and Jacques, of whose existence Aunt Marian and Uncle Max were fortunately unaware, had been one of many. Clare had teetered on the edge of disaster on a number of occasions—Andrea recalled with a shudder an abortive plan to move in with a pop singer shortly before her mercurial cousin had taken off for Paris—and it was a miracle that she hadn't been involved in more than one set of unsavoury headlines before now.

And yet for all her wildness, there was something very sweet about Clare. At times, she could be almost touchingly naïve and trusting, and Andrea had often consoled herself over Peter's dullness with the thought that his reliability and worthiness might be the shield from her worse self that Clare needed.

She was brought back to earth with a start as the drawing door opened and Aunt Marian came out.

'So there you are, dear. Clare is naughty to keep you all to herself. Max has gone to bed early, and I've no one to drink my chocolate with. Come and keep me company.'

Andrea complied with less than her usual willingness. Aunt Marian was no fool, and she was not convinced of her own ability to keep her inner disturbance to herself. She sank down on to one of the luxurious sofas and took the cup she was handed.

'Have you been talking weddings?' Aunt Marian busied herself with the tall silver pot. 'Max said today he was thankful that Clare was our only daughter. He didn't think he could bear to live through all this uproar a second time.' She smiled across at Andrea affectionately. 'But he'll make an exception for you, dear. When can we start planning your wedding?'

Andrea smiled back constrainedly. 'Oh, there's no one at the moment—no one serious anyway,' she said. 'I think Uncle Max has a few more years of peace ahead of him still once Clare is off his hands.'

'Hmm.' Aunt Marian's eyes studied her for a moment,

taking in the slim yet rounded figure, the creamy skin and the soft, vulnerable girl's mouth. 'I don't understand today's young men at all. When I was a girl, you'd have been snapped up in your first season.'

Andrea sighed. 'Maybe I don't want to be snapped up,' she pointed out. 'I do have a career.'

'Yes, I know.' Aunt Marian's tone made it clear what she thought about careers. 'I'm just thankful that Clare seems settled at last. I can speak frankly to you, dear, and I think you know how worried your uncle and I have been over the past two years. We've never wanted to interfere—to stop her living her own life, but there have been times when I've been so frightened for her—frightened that she'd take some disastrous step that she wouldn't be able to recall. Some of the men she's been involved with ...' Aunt Marian shuddered slightly. Her eyes looked shrewdly at Andrea. 'I know you don't think Peter is very exciting, dear, but he'll be so good for Clare, believe me he will.'

Andrea forced a smile. 'Yes, I do believe it. I just wish that he was a little more ...' she paused, searching for the right word.

'Demonstrative,' her aunt supplied. 'I thought so too at first, but now I'm not so sure these outward displays of affection mean a great deal. Clare seems perfectly happy with the situation. She says Peter is shy, and she may be right. It would certainly explain his rather stiff manner sometimes.'

'Perhaps you're right,' said Andrea, setting her cup down on the small table in front of her. 'How is Uncle Max?'

'Behaving very well—avoiding stress and doing what he's told,' his wife said affectionately. 'And Clare's happiness has helped his peace of mind as well. He's even talking of giving up the board altogether and retiring early. He would like to have more time to devote to his charity work, and I'm all for it.' She lowered her voice. 'I don't suppose I should be telling you this, but there's talk of a knighthood in the next Honours list—something he's always dreamed of.'

'But that's wonderful!' Andrea forgot other worries momentarily in her pleasure for her uncle who had given so much of his time for children's charities in recent years. 'And of course, I won't mention it to a soul. Is it definite?'

'Almost, I would say,' her aunt conceded smilingly. 'As long as nothing happens to spoil it for him.' She sighed. 'That's one of the reasons I'm so delighted about Clare. Your uncle's very old-fashioned in some ways, you know, and he has very strong views on the honours system and all it stands for. He wouldn't countenance anything that might bring it into disrepute. And I've always known that if Clare had ever done anything really—foolish, something that might cause a public scandal—these gossip columnists can be quite unscrupulous, dear—then he wouldn't accept the knighthood.'

'You can't be serious.' Andrea stared at her aunt, her brows wrinkled frowningly. 'Uncle Max can't still regard himself as responsible for Clare's dottiness. She's a grown woman.'

Aunt Marian gave a slight smile. 'If she were a grandmother, I don't think it would alter his attitude in the slightest degree. He doesn't approve of this decline in morals they talk about. He feels people in public life should set an example—he always has done.' She sighed. 'Of course, I've never breathed a word of this to Clare herself. I didn't want to burden her with that kind of responsibility, but I don't know whether I was right. Anyway, she's found Peter, so I no longer have any worries on that score.'

Andrea looked at her aunt for a long moment, registering the air of serenity that hung almost tangibly about her. Could she really sit back and see that destroyed? she thought despairingly. Clare was a fool, but marriage to Peter might be the salvation of her, after all.

She got up, forcing a smile.

'Excuse me, will you? I've just remembered—there's something I have to tell Clare.'

Andrea pulled the car into the side of the road, applied the brakes and sat for a moment with her eyes closed. Then she twisted round in her seat and stared back grimly, assimilating almost with disbelief the road she had just ascended.

The late October sun hung low over the valley, and she could see the road like a thin white ribbon winding along the valley side, disappearing at intervals into sheltering clumps of bare trees. On one side of her there had been a towering wall of forbidding black rock, on the other an unfenced drop down to the gleam of the river far below her. She was thankful that the long drive from Paris had given her a chance to at least familiarise herself with the car before she was faced with these conditions, and she had clung to the wheel with grim determination as she mounted through a succession of hairpin bends, praying she would not meet anything coming in the opposite direction.

She looked at the heavy clouds massing in the west and grimaced. All during the drive, the weather had been perfect—golden and autumnal. She had put to the back of her mind all the things she had heard about Auvergne—a place of storms, she'd read somewhere, where the weather was eternally in conflict with itself. Judging by those clouds, war would soon be declared once again!

She reached for her road map and sat studying it, her brows furrowed slightly. Blaise Levallier was making few concessions to his future wife, she thought, asking her to make her own way to this inaccessible place. In itself, this seemed to contain an element of warning, silently conveying the amount of courage and self-sufficiency it would require to survive in this bleak mountain region with its dead volcanoes, and buildings that seemed to have been hewn from solid lava. Yet, in spite of her nervousness, Andrea had to acknowledge its strange compelling beauty. And of course, she told herself, she was not going to be asked to survive here. She gave a slight mischievous grin as she imagined what Clare, a nervous driver at the best of times, would have said when confronted with the valley road she had just traversed. That might have been one way of solving the problem, she thought, stifling her mirth. How would the unknown Blaise Levallier have coped with a bride who applied her handbrake and stubbornly refused to budge? Anyone as determined as he seemed to be would probably have hired a tractor from one of the hill farms and had her dragged to St Jean des Roches.

She sobered slightly as she put her map away. She had only a few kilometres to go to her destination, and the thought was singularly unappealing. A warning voice inside her seemed to be saying it still wasn't too late to turn the car around and drive back to the comparative sanity of Clermont-Ferrand. She could leave the car there and get a train back to Paris. If Clare had been her sole consideration in all this, she might just have done it, she thought as she re-started the car.

She had made that brutally clear to Clare as well, not just that first night when she had reluctantly agreed to go to St Jean des Roches in her cousin's place, but during the subsequent discussions that had taken place. Clare seemed convinced that the incriminating papers would be quite easy to find, but Andrea was not so sure.

'Ask to see them,' Clare had suggested. 'Say you're not too sure about the wording—oh, you'll think of something.'

'I'll have to,' Andrea conceded rather drily.

She had read Blaise Levallier's letters, especially the last one, a dozen times, until she felt every word was imprinted on her memory, and as she read, a slow anger was kindled. Who was this man who thought he could threaten the people she loved and damage their happiness and well-being with impunity? He was simply not going to get away with it. Clare might have been an utter fool, but at least she had seen the error of her ways in time, and he should have had the decency to release her from the ludicrous promise she had made him when she asked him to. Was he so unfeeling that the thought of life with a girl he had literally forced into marriage and for whom he could have no emotional attachment could actually seem tolerable?

If so, his reasons for wanting this hasty marriage must

be extremely cogent ones. She had questioned Clare closely about them, but Clare had destroyed the earlier correspondence with him long ago, and was aggravatingly vague about their contents. She maintained, however, that he had not been at all specific, except about the urgency of his need for a wife at least on paper. That he had said it was 'a legal necessity' was almost all Clare could recall. Andrea had brooded about those words, but they still conveyed very little to her. She had also tried to probe further into the reasons for Martine's family's strong disapproval of their distant cousin, but she'd met with no more success here. The most Martine's parents had let drop were veiled hints, Clare said. But if he regularly made a habit of blackmailing people to get his own way, he was far from being a desirable connection for the eminently respectable Montcours, Andrea thought.

The more she considered what lay ahead of her, the more her apprehension grew. She must be as crazy as Clare to imagine she could get away with this. Just what kind of a man was she going to find waiting for her at St Jean des Roches? she asked herself. Apart from being simply undesirable, had he been guilty of some crime, that he was so reluctant to show his face in more civilised places, and had to find himself a wife by correspondence? And if he was such a villain, what chance did she have to outface him? Andrea sighed. It had never seemed more certain that she was heading for big trouble, but she seemed to be committed now. If she did not arrive at the chateau, Blaise Levallier would undoubtedly set enquiries in train as to her whereabouts, and this would lead to all the problems she had come here precisely to obviate. No, she had to go on. Get in, get the papers, and get out, she told herself. In theory it sounded simple.

She groaned slightly as the first raindrops spattered against the windscreen, and set the wipers in motion. That was all she needed—a strange road, and a rainstorm.

She wondered what Blaise Levallier had thought when he received Clare's meek letter, accepting his terms and telling him the date of her arrival. They had expected some kind of response, probably gloating, but there had been none. She had half hoped that the promised car would not be at the airport so that she would have a golden excuse to take the next plane back to London, but her hope had not been fulfilled. Blaise Levallier might waste no time on unnecessary letters, but his arrangements were efficient enough.

One of the major difficulties confronting her was that she had little idea precisely how much Clare had disclosed about herself during this brief early correspondence she had had with this stranger. It was fortunate that she and Clare had always been on such close terms, she thought, but she still felt anxious. Once again, Clare's memory had been vague, but she insisted that she had not mentioned her parents, or her background. Her letters had concentrated more on the good time she was having in Paris. Andrea wrinkled her nose. Clare's idea of a good time was not always hers, she reflected, and she would have to explain away any discrepancies with the excuse of a poor memory. She also realised that Clare's personality emerged through her letters to a certain extent, and that she would have to act a part for some of the time at least. It was an unnerving thought, but she told herself that if she was very lucky, she might have completed her task and got away from the chateau before any potentially embarrassing explanations or situations arose.

It was suddenly much darker, the friendly sun hidden now by the threatening clouds, and in the distance she heard a low rumble of thunder, curling away. It's a good job I'm not superstitious, she thought, or I might think it was an omen.

The rain had settled to a steady downpour by the time she reached St Jean des Roches some half an hour later, and her neck and shoulders ached from the concentration needed to hold the car on the winding and unfamiliar road.

The village looked little different from others she had passed through on the way, a huddle of houses around a main square with a central fountain. A pale-washed campanile reared itself towards the lowering skies. Beyond the square, the road led upwards again at a gradient which set her nerves twitching. Whoever had christened this place had not been mistaken, she thought. The village itself seemed to have been literally carved out of the side of a rock and she supposed the chateau must be perched dizzily at its summit, somewhere above her.

Her headlights picked out a building of sorts ahead of her and she slowed, peering through the windscreen, uncertain that she had reached the right place. It appeared to be a gatehouse, arching over the road, but the gates themselves were missing, she realised as she drove cautiously through the narrow opening.

For a moment, she thought her lights picked out a face at one of the gatehouse windows, staring down at her, and then her attention was totally diverted by what lay ahead of her. She braked and switched off the engine. Then she sat, staring around at the scene illuminated before her. Slowly and incredulously, she thought, 'But it can't be true ... this can't be the place!'

A chateau in Auvergne, Clare had said, but the picture she had formulated in her mind bore no resemblance to this—ruin she was faced with. How many years of neglect had been needed to produce this effect? she wondered as her eyes wandered over the dark bulk of the building, and the graceful pepperpot tower which rose at one side of it like something from a mediaeval fairytale. There had been a wing once, jutting from the other end of the building, opposite to the tower, but much of it seemed now to consist merely of tumbled masonry. And the main building was dilapidated in the extreme. There were tiles missing from the sloping roof, and on the first floor, some shutters hung crazily from the windows.

She tried to tell herself it was a mistake, and that no one actually lived there, but a thread of smoke hanging above one of the chimneys told her she was mistaken.

Andrea felt anger rising slowly within her. How dared

anyone have let this little jewel of a place decay like this? she thought wildly. And was this really where Blaise Levallier expected gay, comfort-loving Clare to live through the bitter Auvergne winter? It would be like asking a hothouse orchid to flourish at the North Pole. She switched off her lights as if the sudden darkness that descended could also obliterate the reality.

Could he, when he had traced Clare, have learned that she was a considerable heiress? Was this why he had tried to force through their strange marriage so high-handedly? Perhaps Clare's money was intended to restore all this crumbling glory of the past. A sudden gust of anger overcame her and with it a new determination to outwit this man, and she slammed down her hand on the horn, waking the echoes with its blare.

For a moment nothing happened, then the great central door swung open and a woman appeared carrying an enormous black umbrella. Andrea watched her for a moment as she struggled across the weed-strewn courtyard, avoiding the puddles that had rapidly collected in the broken flagstones, then, setting her chin, she collected her handbag and threw open the driver's door.

The wind had risen, she realised, as a sudden gust caught at her, dragging her hair free of the chiffon scarf which confined it at the nape of her neck. She had to catch hold of the car to steady herself.

'*Mademoiselle*!' The woman had reached her side and was struggling to hold the umbrella over her head. '*Permettez-moi. Je vous souhaite bienvenue à* St Jean des Roches.'

Somewhat faintly, Andrea murmured her thanks, and found her hand tucked firmly through the woman's arm. Is she frightened that I'll blow away, or run? she wondered as they started off across the courtyard, heads bent against the stinging rain. As they reached the open door, Andrea remembered something.

'Oh, my case!' She turned to go back for it, but the woman tugged at her insistently, mouthing something at her. Andrea could not make out precisely what she said, but she gathered that someone named Gaston would be delighted to fetch her case for her at a later time, but that now Monseigneur was waiting.

And we can't have that, can we? Andrea thought caustically as she went into the chateau.

The door led directly into what Andrea surmised had originally been the Great Hall of the chateau, but which now shared in the general air of dilapidation. Her first comprehensive glance took in an enormous fireplace, chill and empty, dominating one wall. A table carrying a large old-fashioned oil lamp had been placed against another, and a case of guns hung above it. A few threadbare rugs which might once have been valuable covered the stone floor.

The huge umbrella was quickly shaken free of surplus water and deposited back in a stand beside the main door, holding in addition a number of walking sticks. Then the woman turned to Andrea with a beaming smile, introducing herself as Madame Bresson, the housekeeper. Having said it, she gazed round the hall and gave a deep sigh—as if aware that their surroundings were not a great advertisement for her capabilities, Andrea thought with faint amusement. She herself felt it would take an army of Madame Bressons to restore the chateau to anything approaching its former glory. As she crossed the hall in the housekeeper's wake, she noticed that the tapestry seat covers on several of the high-backed chairs standing against the walls were worn into holes.

One wave of the magic Weston money wand, and the whole chateau will turn back into a pumpkin, she thought angrily.

They stopped outside a heavy door, its timbers pitted with age and wear. Madame Bresson knocked briskly and pushed the door open almost in the same gesture, then motioned encouragingly for Andrea to precede her into the room.

Andrea swallowed, her hands clenching themselves involuntarily into fists at her side, then she stepped across the slightly raised threshold.

It was a much smaller room, the walls panelled from floor to ceiling, and while shabby it presented some appearance of comfort. The large table occupying its centre had been set with a white cloth and cutlery, and a fire had been kindled in the wide fireplace.

A man was standing at the fireplace, one arm resting on the ornate stone overmantel. He was tall, Andrea saw, and slim to the point of leanness with long legs thrust into well-polished riding boots. She assimilated thick black hair, unwaving and rather longer than was strictly fashionable, and a dark arrogant face, high-nosed and hard-mouthed. Whatever she had expected, it hadn't been this, she found herself thinking confusedly. When she had tried to picture her unknown adversary, it had been a much older man who had dominated her mind's eye—thick-bodied and debauched. This man was in his late thirties, if she was any judge, and undeniably attractive.

Then he swung round to face her fully, and Andrea could not control her gasp of dismay. The proud face was marred, perhaps irrevocably, by the long scar which twisted the corner of his left eye and distorted the clean line of the high cheekbone. And even as she thought savagely, Damn Clare for not telling me, the realisation dawned that Clare could not have known.

Was this why Blaise Levallier had felt bound to carry out his wooing, such as it was, by letter? she wondered dazedly, and crushed away the instinctive feeling of compassion that accompanied the thought. The last thing this man wanted would be pity, especially from her.

As if he could guess what she was thinking, he paused a few feet away from her, a faint derisive smile curling the firm lips. His eyes were as dark and hard as the volcanic rocks under his feet as he looked her over.

'*Mon amour!*' Could she detect a note of mockery in the timbre of that low-pitched, slightly husky voice? 'So you've come to me at last.'

Too shocked to protest, she felt long arms drawing her inexorably towards him. She closed her eyes instinctively as the scarred face approached hers. She felt as if she was in a dream, and then dreams were dispelled for ever by the devastating reality of his mouth on hers.

CHAPTER TWO

FOR one suffocating moment Andrea felt the hard pressure of his muscular body against hers. The sound of the closing door behind her, signalling the departure of Madame Bresson, jerked her back to her senses, and she tore herself free of his arms, facing him with flaming cheeks.

'That was not part of the agreement.' She wanted to sound cool and in control of the situation, but to her annoyance her voice came out high and breathless like a little girl's. Anyone would think she had never been kissed before in her life, she thought vexedly.

He shrugged, and again she was aware of that faint amusement.

'Yet it was the reaction expected of us, and it is dangerous to ignore the conventions on these occasions. Our—arrangement is a private one. I imagine you do not wish it to become a matter for speculation in the village.'

She bit her lip. 'No, of course not. I—I wasn't thinking. You—you rather took me by surprise.'

'*Evidémment*,' he murmured. 'I shall have to signal my intentions more clearly in future.'

Now how would Clare react to that? Andrea wondered confusedly. Coquettishly, probably, knowing her. But it was not a response she would dare to try with this man. His scarred face was unimportant. There was about him a kind of sensual magnetism which transcended ordinary physical appeal. Yet she should be able to handle him. She was used to working with men, treated as their equal. Any emotional involvements there had been, she had kept on the lightest possible level.

For one crazy moment she thought, 'I'm frightened of him—frightened of what he could make me feel emotionally.' And then a warning shutter came down in her mind, telling her that she was being nonsensical, and that her senses were playing tricks because she was overtired after the drive.

'Did the journey cause you any problems?' he asked, and it occurred to her that he spoke excellent English. She recalled that Clare had mentioned something about him having possibly spent some time abroad.

'No. It's not the first time I've driven on the Continent.' She sounded impossibly stilted, she thought.

'Perhaps not, but you did not give me the impression that you were totally confident in your driving ability.'

That was her first slip, Andrea told herself furiously. She might have known Clare would probably have poured out her numerous driving mishaps. She had a knack of making them sound feminine and absurd.

She shrugged slightly, making herself smile. 'Well, I didn't actually *kill* anyone on the way.'

'God is merciful.' The scarring gave him the look of a satyr, it occurred to her. 'Permit me to take your coat.'

She tensed involuntarily as his hands came down on her shoulders, but this time his touch was as impersonal as she could have wished.

A heavy wooden settle stood on one side of the fireplace and he invited her to take a seat on it with a wave of his hand. He remained standing.

'Dinner will not be long.' He glanced at his watch. 'Would you care for an *aperitif*, or would you prefer to go to your room before the meal is served?'

'I'm quite glad to be sitting still,' she said frankly. 'Besides, my cases are still in the car.'

'Ah, yes. You will wish Gaston to fetch them.' He tugged at a frayed tapestry bell pull hanging at the side of the fireplace and a bell jangled faintly in the distance. He walked over to the massive, heavily carved sideboard against one wall and picked up a bottle, turning to her with raised eyebrows. 'Dubonnet? Or do you prefer sherry?'

'Dubonnet will be fine,' Andrea said rather helplessly. The situation was fast slipping out of her control. Here she was having a pre-dinner drink with this man as if he was merely her courteous host and nothing more. It was unthinkable that they were going to spend the evening mouthing a lot of polite nothings at each other. There was so much she needed to know. First and foremost it was essential to discover if there was any likelihood of him voluntarily relinquishing his plan to marry Clare even at this late stage. She glanced up with a shy word of thanks as he handed her the drink, and registered the bitter, almost brooding look he wore, and the hard lines of his chin and mouth. He did not look the sort of man who could be easily persuaded about anything, she thought uneasily.

'We'll drink a toast.' Once again she was aware of that quiet element of mockery. 'To our—better acquaintance, *mademoiselle*.'

She murmured something indistinguishable as he touched his glass to hers, and hoped he would blame the heat of the fire for the sudden colour which tinged her face. It was a relief when the door opened and a short stocky man with a brown weatherbeaten face and round, rather staring eyes ambled in.

'*M'sieur?*'

'Ah, Gaston.' Blaise Levallier turned to him, and spoke a few quiet words in his own tongue. Then he turned to Andrea.

'He will need your keys, *mademoiselle*.'

She hesitated a moment, oddly reluctant to part with them. The car was her passport to safety, after all, and it gave her a sense of security to know that its keys were in her keeping.

'You need not worry. Gaston is simple, it is true, but he is also completely trustworthy and devoted to my family.' Blaise Levallier sounded ironic. 'He is perfectly capable of rescuing your baggage and taking it to your room, I promise you.'

She flushed more hotly, annoyed that she was unable to justify her hesitation. She delved into her handbag and produced the key-ring, dropping it into Gaston's waiting palm, murmuring her thanks.

When the door had closed behind him, Blaise Levallier said, 'He speaks no English, I should warn you, but I don't think you will have any difficulty in making him understand you. Madame Bresson—Clothilde—is his aunt and has cared for him since he was a child. He helps with some of the heavy work around the chateau, and assists the herdsmen with the cattle. He is magnificent with the beasts and with the horses. He has a skill born of instinct.'

She nodded constrainedly and sipped her drink. It was essential, of course, for the future mistress of the chateau to be acquainted with these details, but it was a far cry from all she really needed to know. For a moment she found herself wondering how Clare would have reacted to Gaston. Her cousin had an undue sensitivity about all forms of abnormality, and would have had difficulty in adapting herself even to Blaise Levallier's scarred face, she realised.

'What—other help do you have?'

'Very little, as you must have noticed, in the house. The land, of course, is different. But there we all work for each other.'

She looked up at him in surprise, and he explained.

'In my forefathers' day, the chateau took the best of everything—the best of the grazing, the most sheltered portions of the orchards, the finest sites for the vineyards. It has been a policy that has bred poverty and resentment—both forces for destruction. Well, I prefer to construct, rather than destroy, so we have pooled our land and our resources and formed a co-operative. The time is past when the village could simply produce enough food and wine for its own needs and ignore the rest of the world. We make excellent wine—it needs a wider market. In time, too, we will have one of the finest breeding herds in Auvergne.

St Jean des Roches will not become a dead village peopled by the elderly.'

'And what part do you play in this—co-operative?'

'I am its overall manager.' He noted the rather satirical look Andrea sent him, and raised his hand. 'Not because the feudal system still flourishes, I promise you. If I did not have the necessary skill, I would be labouring in the fields. I've served my apprenticeship in management on the plantations of Martinique and—other places.' His smile jeered at her suddenly. 'So if you thought you had come here merely to play the gracious chatelaine, *ma mie*, I'm afraid you must think again.'

'I thought nothing of the sort,' she said truthfully, and relaxed as a knock at the door signalled the arrival of Madame Bresson with their dinner.

Andrea had not realised how hungry she was until Madame lifted the lid off the earthenware pot in the middle of the table and disclosed the simmering *cassoulet*, chunks of pork, slices of country sausage and black-eyed beans swimming in a rich gravy, redolent of garlic and herbs. She made a token protest at the huge plateful that was put in front of her, and then ate every mouthful, assisting it on its way with wedges of fresh, warm bread. The wine they drank was one of the local vintages, Blaise told her, and she found it surprisingly mellow and full-bodied. She refused the cheese that followed, but accepted a cup of strong, black coffee.

'So Clothilde's cooking is to your liking?' Blaise Levallier leaned back in his chair, watching her.

'Very much,' she agreed. 'If I stayed here very long, I'd be as fat as . . .' Her voice tailed away, as she realised with horror what she had just said.

'It will be a metamorphosis that I shall observe with interest,' he said smoothly, as if unaware of her slip.

Well, it was said, and it could not be unsaid, and now was the time, if ever, for her challenge to him.

She set her coffee cup back in its saucer very carefully.

'Monsieur Levallier, I think you must realise as well as

I do that this—this marriage cannot take place.'

'You are incorrect, *mademoiselle*. I realise nothing of the sort.'

She heard the grimness in his voice, but persevered. 'I—I agreed because I was—emotionally disturbed at the time. You can't really intend to hold me to a promise made under such circumstances.'

'Oh, but I can,' he said almost idly, 'and I will. Make no mistake about that, *ma mie*.'

'But it would be too cruel,' she said, her voice quivering, and shrank back from the sudden fury that glared at her from his eyes.

'And do you imagine life has been so kind to me, that I am prepared to take that into consideration?' he demanded harshly, his fingers straying as if in spite of himself towards his damaged face. 'Spoiled from your cradle, what can you know of cruelty?'

'Do I have to learn my first lesson from you?' she flung at him, forgetful in that moment that it was not for herself that she spoke.

He shrugged. 'The nature of the lesson will be your own choice, *mademoiselle*. But I warn you now, the marriage will go ahead as planned. It has already been delayed too long.'

'Am I ever to be told why it's so essential for you to be married?'

He poured himself another cup of coffee. 'You have never displayed any particular curiosity before,' he reminded her drily. 'You seemed more preoccupied with your own—affairs. But there is no reason for you not to know. I am shortly to assume the guardianship of my nephew, and the terms of my brother's will stipulate that I have to be a married man in order to do so. That is all.'

'That's quite enough!' The breath left Andrea's body in a gasp. So Clare was not merely to have been pitchforked into matrimony but into motherhood by proxy as well, she thought furiously. The nerve of this creature! 'Why on earth did your brother include this—stipulation, if he knew you were a bachelor?'

'At the time the will was made, I was expecting to be married—quite soon,' he said, and there was a note in his voice that made her stomach constrict nervously. Her eyes went involuntarily to his scarred cheek, and he nodded sardonically. 'You are very perceptive, *mademoiselle*. And more skilful at concealing your revulsion than my fiancée.' He laughed shortly, without mirth. 'It was a memorable few hours of my life. In the space of a day, I lost everyone in the world I most cared for. My nephew alone remains, and him I do not intend to lose.'

'But surely, if you're his only relative ...'

'But I am not,' he cut in. 'He has an aunt on his mother's side. Unless I fulfil the conditions of the will, she intends to contest the guardianship in the courts. All my money has been sunk into this co-operative. I cannot afford to fight her.'

'But how old is this child? Wouldn't he perhaps be better with his aunt?' Andrea began, and quailed under the look he sent her.

'No, he would not,' he said briefly. 'The child is my heir and his place is here, with his heritage.'

'But what if you have a child of your own ...' Andrea said unthinkingly, and crimsoned as she realised the implication in her words.

'Aren't you afraid I might take you at your word?' His eyes appraised her with sudden insolence. 'What would you do, I wonder? What is that saying you have—close your eyes and think of England, or in this case, France?'

She pressed her hands to her burning face. 'I didn't mean ...' she stumbled, and his smile widened unpleasantly.

'I believe you, *mademoiselle*. Don't look so frightened. I would not demand a sacrifice of that magnitude. I am well aware that my—face would give nightmares to any woman forced to share my bed.'

She shrank from the bitterness implicit in his words. Someone—his fiancée?—must have said that, or something very like it, to him. It betrayed a lack of sensitivity and compassion that was almost inconceivable. Whoever this girl had been, he was well rid of her, she found herself thinking stormily, and checked herself sharply. No matter where her sympathies might instinctively lie, he was still her adversary.

She tried reason again. '*Monsieur*, you've been hurt, I know, but is that any reason to hurt in your turn? This—marriage would be a total disaster. We—we don't know each other. What kind of a relationship could we have?'

Again she was conscious of that uncanny feeling that she was pleading not for Clare but for herself, and she shivered slightly.

'You are cold? Come and sit by the fire.' He got up and strode to the fireplace, flinging on a couple of logs from the basket that stood in the hearth.

'I'm all right here, thank you,' her voice faltered a little and he looked at her impatiently.

'What are you frightened of? This relationship that is only a figment of your own imagination? All I require, *mademoiselle*, is a marriage on paper that will satisfy the lawyers and release Philippe into my custody. Once that has been achieved, you are free to go or stay as you please.'

'But you can't use me like this . . .' she began hotly.

His eyes flashed. 'You did not display the same aversion to using me to heal your pride over your broken love affair, *ma mie*. You were almost brutally frank on the subject. What was it you called me—a lifeline? You cannot now complain if that lifeline becomes a chain to bind you.'

She rose to her feet, pushing her hair back with a weary gesture.

'I—I think I'd like to go to my room,' she said. 'I'm rather tired.'

'Certainly. I will ring for Clothilde.' He reached for the bell rope. Then he turned and walked back to her and stood looking down at her. 'Sleep well,' he said abruptly. 'Perhaps everything will seem a little better in the morning, *hein*?'

She shook her head, suddenly unable to think of a single thing to say in reply.

For a moment he too was silent, looking down at her,

and then almost casually he raised his hand and brushed one finger across her parted lips in a gesture that was almost more intimate than the kiss he had greeted her with on her arrival. She made herself stand her ground, refusing to allow herself to recoil in case he misinterpreted it as an act of repulsion. Whereas, if she was honest with herself, the opposite was true. Why else this almost terrifying tingle of awareness along her nerve-endings? It was a response, the implications of which she did not care to study too closely, and she was thankful when a tap on the door heralded the arrival of Madame Bresson.

The interior planning of the chateau was an architect's nightmare, Andrea thought resignedly as she was led by the housekeeper up a winding stone staircase to the first floor. She found herself in a long, draughty passage at one end of which were a pair of imposing double doors. Andrea gathered from Madame Bresson that that was the chateau's main bedroom, and was presumably occupied by the master of the house.

Her own room, she discovered with amusement and an odd sense of relief, lay in the opposite direction, and at a considerable distance. It was an altogether cosier apartment than she had anticipated, with a small fire burning on the hearth, and enormous old-fashioned furniture which gave a sense of reassurance. The bedstead too was massively constructed in oak, and Andrea wondered with a sinking heart whether the mattress would match it, but a surreptitious poke at it while Madame Bresson was making up the fire soon reassured her.

It was as Madame was wishing her a smiling '*Bonne nuit*' that a thought occurred to her. 'Oh—my keys!'

Madame raised her eyebrows in puzzled enquiry and Andrea elaborated. 'The car keys. I gave them to Gaston so that he could fetch my cases, and I can't see them anywhere.'

The housekeeper's smile broadened. In a daze Andrea heard herself being advised to remain tranquil as Gaston would no doubt have given the keys to Monseigneur, who would arrange its return to the company it had been hired from. Mademoiselle, Madame added triumphantly, was not to concern herself. Monseigneur would arrange everything.

I bet he will, Andrea thought inwardly as the door closed behind Madame. She sank down on the edge of the bed with a feeling of desperation. She had relied so totally on having the car at her disposal for even a few days. Now she would have to depend on what the local bus service had to offer to get her away from this place.

She walked over to the fireplace and sank down on to the rug, holding out her hands to the comforting flames. Not for the first time, she bitterly regretted that she had ever become involved in this charade. Just for a moment she seriously contemplated finding her way back downstairs and telling Blaise Levallier the truth, throwing herself on his mercy, then she dismissed the thought, remembering how he had rejected her accusation that he was cruel.

She squared her shoulders slightly. No, there was little of the milk of human kindness left there, she told herself, and he deserved everything that was coming to him. If Clare's foolish letter was in the chateau she would find it somehow and—Monseigneur could find another dupe to play his marriage game with him.

She gave a little shiver, and wondered why she did so. And at the same time, the thought occurred to her that the sooner she could get away from the chateau—and its master—the better it would be for her.

It rained again in the night. Andrea's first intimation of the fact came when she was rudely awoken by water dripping on her face. Still half asleep, she dragged herself upright and lit the lamp beside her bed, spilling some of the matches as she did so. She stared upwards with mounting indignation as she registered the spreading patch of damp on the ceiling above the bed. She scrambled out of bed and tugged and manoeuvred the heavy bedstead a few inches to the right. Then she fetched the basin from the washstand and placed it to catch the water. There was no point in allowing the water to ruin yet another ceiling below, she thought crossly.

The fire was out, a pile of grey ash, and outside the wind had got up. Somewhere one of the broken shutters was banging monotonously each time a gust took it, and Andrea got back into bed feeling chilled and thoroughly out of temper. Between the sound of drips falling into the china basin and the banging shutter she would be lucky if she closed her eyes again for the rest of the night, she thought.

But it was her inner anxieties, more than exterior conditions, that kept her from sleep, she found. No matter how resolutely she tried to exclude him, the scarred face of Blaise Levallier kept intruding on her interior vision. She told herself she was being ridiculous. After all, he had no real power over her. She was free, white and just over twenty-one. The most she had to fear was his anger when he found out he had been deceived and with any luck she would be well away by then. But all the time, a nagging voice somewhere deep inside her kept telling her that it was not going to be that simple.

She sighed, huddling the fleecy softness of the duvet around her. It would be so easy to get involved, she thought, recalling the pang she had felt when Blaise had spoken of losing everyone he cared for in the space of a few hours. She wondered what had happened. Presumably he was referring to his brother's death, so had the scarring on his face occurred at the same time? It seemed clear there was some connection, and that the subsequent loss of his fiancée was involved in the same web of bitterness.

She closed her eyes, willing her thoughts to be silent, but they would not obey. She found herself speculating about the girl Blaise had been engaged to. Somehow she imagined her small and blonde with a piquant face, like Clare. Was this because in her heart she knew her thoughtless cousin might well have reacted to his damaged face with the same selfish cruelty?

Intuitively, she knew that the visible scars were not the

worst that Blaise Levallier carried. Shuttered behind that bleak hostility was a man who had once laughed and loved and expected to be married and raise a family. Now, as a substitute, he had decided on an emotionless relationship with a stranger, and any hopes for the future were pinned on his orphaned nephew. It was not a healthy situation, she told herself.

There was another puzzling aspect to it, too. Clare had told her and he had confirmed that he had spent much of his life abroad. But if he was the heir to this crumbling property, shouldn't his duty have been to remain here? He had spoken of 'heritage', so obviously he was not indifferent to the fact that he was now lord of this particular manor.

She turned over resolutely, burying her face in the pillow. The linen was old, but had been of the finest quality, and it was charmingly scented with lavender. This was a bed for sweet dreams, not disturbing thoughts, she told herself determinedly, in spite of the leaking roof.

But the dreams which came when she at last fell into an uneasy sleep were as troubling as the thoughts had been. She stood in a ruined church, where stars peeped through the broken roof, and grass grew along the aisles. A man stood at the altar alone, endlessly awaiting a bride who did not come, and it was only when she tried to speak to him to comfort him, to run to him and touch his arm, that she realised that she was invisible, calling to him in a voice he could not hear.

When she awoke to find a ray of watery sunlight finding its way through a crack in the faded brocade curtains at the windows, she found her cheeks wet with tears.

She was angrily brushing the betraying drops away when Madame Bresson knocked at the door, and came in bringing a fresh jug of hot water for the washstand. She clucked distressfully at the sight of the bowl on the floor, and burst into a flood of largely incomprehensible explanations from which Andrea gathered that the majority of the bedrooms suffered in the same way during heavy rain, but that Gaston would be despatched to the roof that very morning to carry out some essential patchwork. After assuring herself that Andrea had everything she needed and could find her way downstairs to the dining room, she withdrew.

Andrea washed and dressed hastily in a pair of denim jeans, topped with a ribbed black polo-necked sweater. She looked about her with critical eyes as she went downstairs. The place was clean, certainly, but it was uncared for. There were some magnificent pieces of furniture, but they were not displayed to their best effect, and there were no flowers to be seen anywhere. She gave a little sigh. There might be no money for structural repairs, if Blaise Levallier was heavily committed to this farming co-operative of his, but it would take a very small outlay to make the interior of the chateau far more pleasant. Covers could be mended, she thought, and it might even be possible with care to dye some of the faded curtains. Then she checked herself abruptly. She had to remember why she was here, she told herself vehemently. The state of the chateau, or any of its occupants for that matter, was none of her concern. She would be better occupied in thinking about how she was going to get hold of Clare's letter.

She was somewhat disconcerted to find Blaise Levallier already seated at the dining table, going through some mail. He did not look any more approachable in the cold light of day, she thought uneasily, as she slid into her place with a murmured greeting.

'I hope you slept well, *mademoiselle.*' The words were civil enough, but the tone of utter indifference in which they were spoken stung Andrea.

'Not particularly.' She shook out her table napkin, and helped herself from the basket of warm *croissants.*

His eyebrows rose. 'You distress me.' His voice was sardonic now. 'May I ask why not?'

'You may.' She spread the *croissant* with jam and bit into it appreciatively. 'The roof above my room leaks.'

He frowned swiftly. 'Then you should naturally not have been given such a room. I will speak to Clothilde.'

'Oh, it isn't her fault.' Andrea reached for the coffee pot

and filled her cup. 'She says all the rooms are the same.'

'Mine is not.'

She gave him a dulcet smile. 'Naturally,' she agreed.

He lifted his cup and drank with a meditative air. 'Then what do you suggest, *mademoiselle*? I hesitate to put forward the obvious solution . . .'

She hated herself for her faint, involuntary blush. 'Naturally,' she repeated, hanging on like grim death to the dulcet smile. 'But you could also get the roof mended.'

He shrugged. 'Gaston does what he can.'

'So I've gathered, but perhaps it's time you got a professional opinion—unless it's your intention to have the house crumble about your ears eventually.' She smiled at him again. 'You'll forgive my frankness, but I do have a vested interest in it now.'

That was good, she thought with satisfaction, and it should help allay any suspicions he might have about her motives. If she could convince him that she had given way to *force majeure* over their marriage, it would make her task very much easier.

'Yes.' He studied her for a moment, and she could sense he was puzzled. 'You are—reconciled to our contract, then?'

'I don't seem to have much choice,' she said, with a slight lift of her shoulders. 'You've made it clear what will happen if I back out, and I couldn't stand that.' She gave an exaggerated shudder.

'So I imagined.' There was a wry satisfaction in his voice. 'It would lead to the sort of publicity that neither of us desires, I am sure, apart from the probable injury to your father's health.'

Andrea, who had just taken a mouthful of coffee, choked and had to replace her cup hastily on its saucer.

'I—I don't know what you mean,' she managed at last.

'No?' His look was bleak. 'I think I make myself perfectly clear, *mademoiselle*. Your father is an eminent man, and the deterioration in his health has caused a great deal of concern in circles with which I am well acquainted. You could not imagine I would make no enquiries about your background.'

She could not very well reply that they had been counting on it, she thought, her heart hammering unevenly.

'I suppose not,' she said at length. 'That was why you knew you could threaten me, of course. Because of—Daddy.'

'Hardly threaten, *ma mie*. I simply pointed out to you what the consequences would be if you failed to fulfil the terms of our agreement, and left the decision to your good sense.'

He was mocking her, she knew, and her resentment hardened.

'I hope you think your victory is worth the means you had to stoop to to win,' she said sharply.

'That remains to be seen.' He finished the coffee in his cup and stood up. 'When you have finished breakfast, I thought you might like to ride with me. As you reminded me, you have a vested interest in the estate now, and you may be interested in the changes we are making.'

She was just about to inform him frankly that the only thing she could imagine worse than a morning in his undiluted company was a morning on horseback, when she remembered with dismay that Clare was a keen rider and had probably mentioned this in her letters. She nearly groaned aloud. She could always invent a headache or some other minor ailment, but this might arouse his suspicions, and this was the last thing she wanted. She could ride, but she had none of Clare's equestrian flair, and she was nervous of horses.

She forced a smile. 'That would be lovely,' she agreed. 'I—I'll just get a jacket.'

'Soit.' He sent her a long look, and for the first time she noticed, inconsequentially, how long his eyelashes were. 'Shall we say then that we will meet at the main door in ten minutes' time?'

As she came downstairs again, Andrea wondered if it would be possible to slip on the stairs and feign a sprained ankle. But as she came round the final curve of the stairs, she saw Blaise Levallier just below her glancing idly through an agricultural catalogue.

He glanced up at the sound of her step. 'Docile—and punctual,' he remarked. 'You will make an admirable wife, *ma mie*.'

She glared at him in impotent silence. Crossing verbal swords with him would get her nowhere, she reasoned, and all past scores would be paid off anyway when she took her departure and he realised he no longer had the proof he needed of his hold over Clare.

She noted ironically that the stables were in much better condition than the house itself, and commented sweetly on the fact.

'Perhaps because I find animals of considerably more value than human beings, *mademoiselle*,' came the immediate retort, and she subsided angrily.

Her heart sank when Gaston led out the mare that Blaise had designated for her to ride. She was a far cry from faithful old Penelope on whose broad back a much younger Andrea had taken her first quaking lessons. She was a sprightly roan, who sidled and jumped and tossed her head, and her bright eyes spoke of mischief.

'She needs exercise,' said her tormentor, already astride his own horse, and looking, Andrea thought bitterly, as if he were part of it.

She looked round for Gaston to help her mount, but he had disappeared back into the stables, so she had to lead the reluctant Delphine over to an ancient mounting block and get herself somehow into the saddle. It was not a polished performance, but at least she found herself on the mare's back, instead of spreadeagled on the ground when it was completed. So far, so good, she thought, her sense of humour aroused by the sheer absurdity of the situation.

If I break my neck, at least it will be one way out of this mess, she told herself philosophically.

But before they had been out for very long, Andrea knew that it was a very different part of her anatomy that was going to suffer. Apart from that, Delphine was proving the handful she had feared and more. Clare had always said that horses could sense who had the mastery, and it was clear that the mare had written her off as an easy touch. She began to take liberties almost as soon as they were out of the stable yard, refusing to respond to Andrea's rather tentative pressure on the reins with a toss of her head, and even swinging aside to eat the grass from the verges at the side of the track. The moment of truth came when a large bird flew out of the hedge immediately in front of her, and she squealed with indignation and reared up, nearly unseating Andrea in the process. Humiliatingly but inevitably, Blaise Levallier was there, grabbing the reins and soothing the mare, at the same time forcing her to compliance.

'Thank you.' Andrea knew her face was crimson.

'It is nothing.' He gave her a narrow look. 'Perhaps it was a mistake asking you to ride so soon. You must still be tired after your journey—and your sleepless night.'

Now why didn't I think of that? Andrea asked herself in exasperation. Aloud she said, 'Probably,' in a wooden voice.

She took a firm grip on herself and the reins after that, determined to cope better. Certainly, in spite of everything, there was a great deal to enjoy. The air seemed to sparkle after the night's rain, and the views as they continued to climb were breathtaking. Away in the distance she could glimpse the flattened cones of the *puys*, the dead volcanic mountains of Auvergne, while around them the trees still wore the last remnants of their autumn glory before the stark onset of winter.

Andrea felt so exhilarated that when they eventually reached a level, grassy stretch of ground she forgot to be nervous when the horses broke into a canter, and then a gallop. Delphine was no longer a monster, fixed on her undoing, but a lovely creature, fluid of bone and muscle, who merely wanted to share her pleasure in her own swift eagerness.

When they reined in, Andrea saw that from this vantage

point it was possible to look down on the village and the chateau. Seen from above, it had an even more forlorn look, and Andrea stole a sideways look at her companion to see his reaction. The scarred side of his face was hidden from her, but his expression was bleak and brooding and she did not dare venture a remark.

At last, when she had begun to think he had forgotten her presence, he said '*Allons!*' in an impatient tone, and they turned the horses and rode on.

The black mood that possessed him persisted as they toured the vineyards, and looked at the new bottling plant which had been installed. Andrea, somewhat to her own surprise, found she was genuinely interested in what was being achieved, and it was frustrating to have her questions answered in monosyllables.

At last she could hold her tongue no longer.

'This ride was your idea, *monsieur*,' she reminded him acidly. 'If you want me to learn about the estate, you need to improve your teaching technique.'

The look he sent her was chilling, but he made no response. She was not altogether surprised, however, when she found they were on their way back to the chateau.

'Here endeth the first lesson,' she observed flippantly.

This time he did reply, and his voice was icy with rage. 'It may all seem a joke to you, *mademoiselle*, from your secure English background, but to me and many others in this village, it is life and death. Do you know how many villages there are in France where old people sit in their houses alone, because their children have left—gone to the cities to find work? Do you even care? I doubt it. But I care. And I care too that my home—the house which my family has occupied for hundreds of years—is falling into a ruin about me. Do you imagine that I would have permitted this neglect? Regard it well, *mademoiselle*. That is what hate can do, and spite and revenge. It is not pretty, *hein*?'

'Whose hate, *monsieur*?'

'My father's, *mademoiselle*. My younger brother was his favourite. He could not forgive me for being the elder and his heir. I could do nothing right—nothing that would please him, except absent myself. He could have stopped the rot then, if he had wished, but he did not wish. I do not think he cared if there was one stone standing upon another when I came into my inheritance. Every last franc was devoted to Jean-Paul, and to our plantation Belle Rivière.'

'Your brother ran the plantation?'

'*Oui.* It was his part of the inheritance. God knows I never grudged it to him. But there were problems. Several bad seasons—hurricanes, pests which destroyed the crop. At last my father ordered me to go there and put things right. It would have taken a miracle. By the time I arrived, Jean-Paul had speculated trying to recoup some his losses, and was facing ruin.'

He stopped abruptly, as if sensing her tension. The anger and bitterness died from his face as if a slate had been wiped clean.

'But I am boring you, *mademoiselle*, with our sordid family squabbles. My father has been dead for two years, God rest his soul, and Jean-Paul and his wife are also at peace now. I am left to salvage what I can and make some kind of life for myself and Philippe.'

She moistened her dry lips, appalled at what he had let her see.

'And Belle Rivière? What has happened to that?'

'The house has gone,' he said briefly. 'It was—burned to the ground a year ago. The land is now leased to the government.'

Something warned her that now was not the time to probe any further. She stole a glance at him and saw that the scar was standing out livid against his tan.

Gaston was waiting to take the horses when they rode into the yard. The ground suddenly looked a long way down, Andrea thought wearily as she eased her aching rear. She felt agonisingly stiff, and was afraid her legs might give way under her through sheer reaction when she dismounted.

'Permit me.' Blaise Levallier appeared at her side. Gratefully, she freed her feet from the stirrups and allowed herself to slide from Delphine's back into his waiting arms. Just for a moment she felt the brush of his warm body against hers, and knew an insane urge to press herself against him, savouring the intimate smell of his sweat.

As her feet touched the ground, she pulled herself away, her face flaming as if he could guess her wanton thoughts, and stumbled slightly.

'Take care.' His voice was courteous but impersonal. 'If you ask Clothilde, she will prepare a hot bath for you. I will see you at dinner.'

He gave her a brief formal nod, before turning and striding away.

Andrea had to force herself not to turn and watch him go. She felt confused and disturbed by this sudden turbulence in her emotions. I hate him, she told herself almost desperately. I've got to hate him. And I must never let him touch me again.

CHAPTER THREE

ANDREA leaned her head against a folded towel, placed strategically over the high back of the huge old-fashioned bath, and closed her eyes with a sigh of relief.

The bathroom to which Madame Bresson had led her was next door to the room containing the massive throne-like lavatory which had reduced her to irreverent giggles the previous evening. It was a chilly apartment, its walls hung with large antique embossed tiles in an attractive scroll pattern. The bath, supported solidly on four large claw feet, stood against one wall, its brass taps gleaming. The wall above was festooned with a motley collection of elderly pipework, which emitted strange groaning noises when the taps were turned on.

Observing the care with which Madame had performed this operation, Andrea surmised that the chateau's plumbing probably possessed a temperament all its own. But she had nothing to complain of in the actual temperature of the water, and the surroundings could be made less Spartan, she thought, mentally boxing in the pipes, and adding a rug to the chill of the tiled floor.

She moved her bruised legs in the cooling water, wincing slightly as she did so. She might be lucky enough to avoid total paralysis, she thought ruefully, but she was going to be very, very stiff. It was to be hoped that she wouldn't find it necessary to run away during the next twenty-four hours, because even quite gentle exercise was probably going to be beyond her.

But she had to admit that her morning in the fresh air had done her good. She was really looking forward to the lunch that Madame Bresson had promised would be served as soon as she was ready.

And after lunch she was presumably free to do as she pleased. Some time she would have to write to Clare, but as yet she had little to report in the way of good news or even progress. Perhaps the letter could be delayed until things became more positive, and she would use the time instead to explore the chateau a little.

It had occurred to her that if Blaise Levallier was managing the co-operative he must have an office of some description, probably in the chateau itself, and that this would be the most obvious place for him to keep his personal correspondence including, presumably, Clare's letter. That was the place she would begin her search. The thought filled her with distaste and she had to remind herself forcibly of the equally distasteful methods Blaise had himself employed to try and force her cousin into marriage.

It was useless to pretend that she had not been shocked into a certain sympathy for him by the morning's revelations. Looking back on the happiness of her own childhood, it seemed incredible that such bitter hostility could exist in a family. It did much to explain the cynical lines that marked his mouth, and the cold ruthlessness he displayed in his dealings with Clare. Yet she could not doubt his affection for his dead brother. There had been no tinge of censure in his references to the problems Jean-Paul had experienced in running the plantation, only regret. His father's favouritism had not had the power to sour that relationship at least. It was clear there was a connection between the loss of the plantation and Jean-Paul's death, and that there was also a link between this tragedy and the scarring of Blaise's face.

She got carefully out of the bath and began to towel herself dry. She must not get involved, she thought, with a sense of desperation. She would not be here for much longer, and when she left, she wanted to be able to turn her back on St Jean des Roches and its master without a second thought or trace of regret. And if a warning inner voice murmured that it might already be too late, she closed her ears deliberately.

Madame Bresson had taken her jeans and sweater to launder, so Andrea changed into a slim-fitting skirt in golden tweed, topped by a dark green woollen shirt, and pinned up her chestnut hair into a neat French pleat.

She lunched on thick home-made broth, savoury with herbs and vegetables, ending her meal with fresh fruit from the chateau's own orchards and local cheese. She was just finishing her coffee when Madame Bresson came to clear the table.

'No, you must let me help you. You have quite enough to do.' Andrea got up gingerly and began to load her dishes on to the tray Madame had brought in spite of the housekeeper's protests. Then she carried the tray to the kitchen. After all, she told herself in justification, if she was really going to be the mistress here, she would be taking over some of the household duties, and her independent spirit rebelled at being waited on.

The kitchen was a large cheerful room with an enormous glowing range, which also provided hot water as well as cooking facilities. In the middle of the room was a large wooden table with a well-scrubbed top, and an array of fearsome-looking knives to hand. Strings of onions and garlic hung from hooks round the walls, and a huge built-in dresser supported an assortment of copper and cast iron utensils. Andrea enjoyed cooking, although she had never embarked on a Cordon Bleu course as Clare had done for a brief period. She thought that once the vagaries of the range had been mastered, any woman could revel in preparing meals in these homely surroundings.

Madame Bresson seemed not to resent her presence in the slightest, but showed a positive eagerness to open the china cupboards and disclose the secrets of the larder and the wine cellar. She grieved openly over the fact that the chateau was not supplied with electricity and Andrea learned, without any real surprise, that this had been one of the decisions of 'Monsieur *le père de* Monseigneur'. She would have loved to know more, but Madame became so tight-lipped at the first of her tentative questions that she desisted.

When she inquired whether anyone would mind if she looked round the chateau, Madame looked a little blank, but she cheered visibly when Andrea assured her, feeling wretchedly guilty, that she did not require a guide, but would be quite happy to look about on her own. Her guilt increased when a large bunch of keys was thrust trustingly into her hands with a beaming smile from the housekeeper.

As she turned to leave, her foot struck something lying on the flagged floor. She bent to retrieve it, and saw to her surprise it was an intricately carved bobbin, the type used in lacemaking.

'Whose is this?' She turned to Madame Bresson, the bobbin extended on her palm.

Madame gave a little cry and slipped the bobbin into her capacious apron pocket, profuse in her thanks. Andrea was intrigued.

'Do you make lace, *madame*?' she asked.

Madame nodded proudly. The lace of Auvergne was justly famous—an ancient tradition passed down from mother to daughter for generations. But *hélas*, there were no daughters for her to pass on her skills to, so Monseigneur was to arrange that she should teach some of the young girls in the village. When Monseigneur was married, she added rather anxiously, he had promised she would have more time to spare for this.

Andrea smothered a smile, guessing this was why Madame had been so ready to introduce her to the inner workings of the establishment.

'Perhaps you'll show me some of your lace when you have time,' she said gently. If she could do so without offending the housekeeper, she thought she might buy something from her—a collar perhaps, or a shawl to take away with her, as a souvenir of what surely would be the strangest few days of her life. It would be a safer reminder than the haunted look in a man's eyes, and the painful memory of the response even his slightest touch could kindle.

Two hours later she was ready to weep with frustration and annoyance. She had explored all the habitable portions of the chateau, tiptoeing through quiet rooms shrouded in dust covers, along winding corridors where pictures of long-dead Levalliers gazed down haughtily on her intrusion, and up and down staircases until her mistreated muscles screamed for mercy. The only room she had hesitated to enter was the bedroom she knew to be Blaise Levallier's. After all, her exploration of the chateau could be attributed to simple feminine curiosity, and an interest in historical houses. But she could think of no convincing reason for being discovered in his bedroom—except one which could invite consequences she did not care to contemplate.

She had developed a slight headache and her throat and nasal passages felt full of dust. Fresh air was what she needed, she thought, dispiritedly shrugging herself into her brown leather driving coat. Something to blow the cobwebs away, literally as well as figuratively, and give her a clear perspective on things. She was beginning to wonder if it wouldn't be best to cut her losses and get out. After all, Clare's own wedding was not too long away, and surely it might be possible to fend Blaise Levallier off until then, and she was lost to him for ever. At the moment she was simply searching for a needle in a haystack. Clare had been a fool, but was she herself any less harebrained for setting out on this wild goose chase? Why couldn't Blaise have been the pompous overbearing oaf she had visualised? There would have been a kind of malicious pleasure in leading someone like that up any number of garden paths. She might even have been tempted to flirt with him. But with Blaise, she felt that all the initiative had been taken out of her hands, and that in some odd way it was he who was dictating the course of events.

She shivered a little as she stepped out of the big main door into the fading afternoon sunlight, thrusting her hands into the pockets of her coat. She supposed that the chateau possessed a garden of sorts, but if it was as neglected as the building, it would probably be like hacking one's way through the jungle. She paused in the middle of the courtyard, looking moodily around her. A sudden feeling of intense irritation came over her and she bent, dragging out a handful of weed and flinging it with more strength than accuracy in the direction of the gatehouse. The muddy bundle thudded against one of the lower windows and slid sadly downwards to rest on the sill, and a matter of seconds later Andrea heard one of the upper windows being opened. Too late she remembered the face she thought she had glimpsed on her arrival, and a hand flew to her mouth in dismay.

There was indeed a face, rather a nice one with a beard and a pair of rimless glasses, gazing down at her with pained astonishment.

'*Pardonnez-moi, mademoiselle. Puis-je vous aider?*' The words might be French, she realised hysterically, but the accent was unmistakably English.

'I—I'm awfully sorry,' she said. 'I—I didn't realise anyone lived there. No one mentioned you, you see.'

'You're English too!' The look of pained astonishment gave way to a beaming smile. 'I say, what a coincidence.

Are you a tourist? You're rather off the beaten track here, you know. This isn't one of the show places.'

'No.' Andrea turned and looked at the chateau, narrowing her eyes against the sun. 'But it could be lovely,' she added, feeling like a mother rushing to defend an ugly child.

'I've got some tea.' His voice became almost conspiratorial. 'Would you like a cup?'

Tea wasn't her most favourite drink, but Andrea could recognise a friendly gesture when she saw one. Besides, the very fact that Blaise Levallier had concealed the fact that one of her compatriots was occupying his gatehouse, presumably with his knowledge and permission, was intriguing. Wild horses wouldn't have dragged her away from the gatehouse now.

The small studded door swung open as she approached. Her host was younger than she had imagined from her first glance, probably only a year or so older than herself. He was of medium height and looked as if his wardrobe of faded jeans, sweater and scuffed suede boots had been purchased at Oxfam.

'Alan Woodhouse,' he introduced himself. She appreciated the firmness of his handshake.

'Andrea Weston.'

'The same initials.' He looked at her solemnly through his glasses. 'We were obviously fated to meet. Do come in. I should watch the stairs—I think they're supporting a family of death watch beetle and damned little else. This way. This is my living room. It's a bit of a mess, I'm afraid, because I do—rather—live in it.'

That, Andrea thought, was an understatement. Her eyes roamed dazedly round the small room, taking in the camp bed with its sleeping bag, the portable stove with its blue gas bottle standing next to it, the wooden crate loaded with tins, and the round table cluttered with crockery in various stages of cleanliness, books, scattered papers and a portable typewriter.

Alan Woodhouse plunged at the table and began to hunt

around. 'I did do some washing up yesterday, actually—or was it the day before? There's no water laid on here, so I fetch it all from the stable yard in a bucket. But I can't complain. He isn't charging me a penny, and if I can't work here, then I don't deserve to get on.'

'Are you a writer?' Andrea lowered herself gingerly on to a rickety stool.

'One day, perhaps. I'm doing research at the moment, for a thesis—the life of Vercingetorix. He came from these parts, you know.'

Memories of schoolday struggles with the classics came back to Andrea. 'Oh, I know. "All Gaul is divided into three parts."'

'Yes.' He looked at her soberly. 'I suppose everyone knows that beginning. But it's the end of the story that's always fascinated me. I must have a soft spot for losers, anyway, and Julius Caesar has always seemed such a cold fish to me. Always so objective and—laconic. I mean, when you think—here's his great enemy, the Gallic chieftain who has defeated his army and withstood a terrible siege, coming out to surrender to him, riding down the hill from Alesia in his golden armour—or that's how the legends describe him. And what does Caesar say?' He dived at a tattered paper-bound book and opened it towards the end. 'Just listen. "He"—that's Caesar talking about himself—"seated himself at the fortification in front of his camp, and there the chiefs were brought; Vercingetorix was delivered up and the arms laid down."' He shook his head. 'Not exactly passionate stuff, is it?'

Andrea laughed. 'Nor was "I came, I saw, I conquered,"' she pointed out. 'But there's an endearing matter-of-factness about it, just the same, a suggestion of the inevitable being bowed to once again. However, I can see why you prefer Vercingetorix. There's a lot to be said for a folk-hero who goes on behaving heroically even when he's lost.'

He smiled delightedly at her. 'That's just what I feel. You've seen his statue, of course, in Clermont-Ferrand. It's an enormous thing. God, this tea! You must be dying of thirst. It's only condensed milk, I'm afraid.'

Andrea suppressed a shudder. 'Lovely,' she said weakly.

But when she took an experimental sip from the steaming mug he handed her, she found it altogether better than she had expected.

Alan dumped himself down on the edge of the camp bed and grinned at her. 'It's marvellous to meet someone else who can speak English. French isn't my strong point, I'm afraid. Of course, Monsieur Levallier speaks English too, but he isn't really the sociable type.'

'No,' Andrea said constrainedly, and he looked up in sudden alarm.

'Oh hell, I haven't put my foot in it, have I? Was it you that drove in last night! Are you staying at the chateau? I suppose you're a friend of his.'

Andrea stared at the floor. 'In a way,' she acknowledged.

There was a prolonged silence and when she looked up, she saw that Alan's ears and as much of his face as remained visible above the beard had turned bright red.

'I didn't mean to pry,' he mumbled, avoiding her glance.

To her annoyance, she found she was blushing in turn.

'You're quite wrong,' she protested. 'I am staying at the chateau, as a matter of fact, but ...' She hesitated, completely at a loss as to how to explain. She couldn't tell him the truth, obviously, but it seemed wrong to involve him in her deception. She decided to compromise. 'I'm here on business, actually. Monsieur Levallier and I have some— negotiations to discuss.'

'Oh.' His face cleared. 'Actually I didn't think ... I mean, you don't look the type. Oh, lord, here I go again! What I'm trying to say is that he's obviously knocked around a hell of a lot. I imagine he'd want someone who could match his own experience. Not that you aren't very attractive,' he added punctiliously.

She had to smile. 'Thank you, kind sir, she said.'

He grinned too. 'Well, you know what I mean,' he said plaintively.

She was nevertheless glad when they deserted personalities and returned to the thesis he was writing, and the local history he had acquired during his stay in the area. She learned that he had been living in the gatehouse for over six weeks, and planned to stay for another month at least.

'Perhaps we could eat out together one evening,' he suggested eagerly. 'I know I look as if I'm living on the breadline, but I do have some money. There's quite a good place at Craudon. Transport's a bit of a problem though. Could we use your car, d'you suppose?'

She looked at him in dismay. 'I—I don't have it any more.'

'Oh.' He digested this for a moment. 'What happened to it?'

'It was a hired car. I think it had to go back to Clermont-Ferrand.'

'Oh, that's a pity,' he said cheerfully. 'But I'm sure we'll get round it somehow. Jean-Luc Gabrier has a motor-bike. He might lend it to us for the evening.'

'Wonderful!' she agreed, wondering faintly how Blaise Levallier would react to the news that his future wife was careering round the countryside on the pillion seat of a borrowed motor-cycle. One thing was certain, it wouldn't be any more uncomfortable than Delphine.

She glanced at her watch and gave a start of dismay.

'Heavens, it's late! I must go.'

'I'll be in touch,' Alan promised. He got up and accompanied her down the stairs to the door. She had started away across the courtyard when she heard him call cheerfully, 'Goodbye, Andrea!'

Oh God, she thought frantically, her stomach churning suddenly. I told him my real name. She swung round and almost flew back to the gatehouse before he could shut the door.

'Hello.' Alan looked at her in surprise. 'Forget something?'

'Yes.' She moistened her lips. 'I—I'd completely forgotten. Do you think you could call me Clare instead?'

He was looking at her as if she was mad, and little wonder, she thought miserably. She went on, improvising desperately, 'I—I don't use my own name—for professional purposes. Monsieur Levallier knows me as Clare. It would only cause confusion if you started calling me something different, and the language problems are bad enough without that.'

The puzzled look vanished, to her relief. Language problems were something Alan could associate with.

'I'll remember.' He looked her over and gave a regretful shake of his head. 'But I don't approve of the change. You're no Clare.'

He could say that again, Andrea thought, as she hurried back across the courtyard. If their roles had been reversed, Clare would have revelled in a situation like this, enjoying the play-acting and the sense of conspiracy.

Madame Bresson was hovering, her face agitated, as Andrea entered the chateau.

'Mademoiselle.' Her voice was reproachful. 'Monseigneur has been asking for you.'

'Oh dear,' Andrea said lightly, taking off her coat. 'Am I going to be shot?'

She walked into the dining room with a jauntiness she was far from feeling. Blaise Levallier was standing by the window smoking a cigarette. He swung round as she entered and his face wore a thunderous frown.

'Where have you been?' he demanded harshly.

'Looking round.' She dropped the bunch of keys Madame had given her on to the table and faced him defiantly.

'It takes so long?' He expelled a cloud of smoke impatiently.

'Why?' she asked with deliberate innocence. 'Have you missed me?'

There was a long silence. Then, 'Have a care, *ma mie*,' he said softly. 'It may seem very entertaining to provoke me, but the consequences might be less—amusing.'

His dark face looked satanic, and it took all the courage she possessed to stand her ground.

'Your threats don't worry me, *monsieur*,' she said untruthfully. 'I have been forced to accept the prospect of our marriage, and nothing could be worse than that.'

'You think not?' His laugh was soft and jeering, but there was a note in it which chilled her. 'Then you still have a lot to learn, *ma chère* Clare, in spite of your much-vaunted sophistication.'

Just what had Clare told him in those letters of hers? she wondered frantically, her hands clenching at her sides in a swift nervous gesture she was sure would not have escaped his gaze.

'And was your exploration of my house as—rewarding as you hoped?' His changes of mood were as unpredictable as the Auvergne weather, she thought exasperatedly. And yet at the same time she had the uneasy feeling that tone of courteous interest concealed something very different. Almost as if he knew exactly what she had been up to and was silently mocking her.

'It was most interesting,' she replied expressionlessly.

'And your visit to the gatehouse? No doubt that was more interesting still.'

So that was what this cat-and-mouse game was all about.

'Quite fascinating, thank you,' she said clearly. 'I'm surprised, however, that you didn't think it was worth telling me that you had a lodger.'

He smiled sardonically. 'Perhaps, *mademoiselle*, I was aware that you were perfectly capable of ferreting out such information for yourself.'

She flushed at the implication in his words, and was glad when the door opened to admit Madame Bresson with a tureen of soup. Madame fortunately seemed totally unaware of the tense atmosphere in the room, and bustled about putting the finishing touches to the dinner table, and uttering motherly adjurations to eat her good soup while it was still hot.

Andrea picked up her spoon. 'I still don't see why you didn't tell me,' she protested. 'You must have known I would be interested in the fact that one of my own countrymen was living on the doorstep.'

He shrugged. 'All the more reason to keep the matter quiet, maybe.'

She slammed the spoon back on to the table. 'Of all the damned nerve . . .' she began heatedly. 'Just what are you implying?'

'That whatever your past indiscretions may have been, *ma belle*, I would prefer the behaviour of the future Madame Levallier to remain—impeccable.'

There was a brief silence. 'You're very insulting,' she said unevenly.

'Why? Because I refer openly to things you have yourself made no secret of?' He glanced at her, brows slightly raised. 'Now calm yourself and eat your soup. You are already too thin.'

'Oh, am I?' She found fresh fuel for her indignation. 'I'm *so* sorry that I don't find favour with you, Monseigneur. No doubt you're a connoisseur in such matters.'

'Don't allow it to distress you, *ma mie*,' he said almost kindly. 'I am sure, without your clothes, you would have a certain appeal.'

'But not to you, of course,' she said, her voice shaking with rage.

'I wasn't aware you wished to appeal to me in that way, *mademoiselle*.' He reached out and poured some wine into her glass. 'However, if you wish to judge my reactions, you could always take your clothes off.'

'And you could go to hell!' She pushed the soup plate away from her, spilling some of its contents on to the white cloth.

'I think I have been there already.' His voice was suddenly so harsh that she was startled out of her anger. There was a long pause, and then he said almost conversationally, as if the last few minutes had never existed, 'And what was your impression of our young historian?'

'He seems to know a fair bit about his subject.' She forced herself to answer in the same vein. 'He soon left me behind—I'm afraid the Gallic Wars weren't a particular strong point of mine at school,' she added hurriedly, *à la mode de* Clare.

'No?' He looked at her sardonically. 'Well, perhaps Roman military tactics have only a limited appeal. But Caesar might have taught you one thing, *ma mie*. We Auvergnats make bad enemies. Maybe you should remember that.'

Andrea did not enjoy her dinner, although the escalopes of veal Madame Bresson served, accompanied by courgettes and potatoes fried with onions, were quite delicious. By the time the housekeeper came to clear the table, her one thought was of escape.

'Where are you going?' Blaise's voice halted her as she made for the door.

'To my room.' There was an unconscious appeal in her hazel eyes as she turned to face him. 'I—I'm rather tired.'

'Sit down, please.' He indicated the settle. 'I want to talk to you.'

What she wanted didn't matter, of course, she thought stormily, but she was too weary to face another battle, so she walked over obediently and seated herself, gazing down into the leaping flames in the hearth.

'What did you want to say to me?' she asked eventually, when he showed no sign of breaking the silence.

'First, I want to give you this.'

She looked up and saw that he was holding out a small velvet-covered box towards her. She took it mechanically and opened it. The ring reposing on the satin bed inside it almost took her breath away. It was obviously very old, and the magnificent ruby which formed its centrepiece was surrounded by diamonds, like glittering petals clinging to some exotic crimson flower.

'What is it?' she gasped.

'It's the betrothal ring of the Levallier family,' he said with a certain impatience. 'Put it on.'

'No.' She closed the lid of the box with fingers that shook.

His eyes narrowed dangerously. 'Have the goodness to obey me.'

'I—I can't wear it.' Her throat tightened convulsively. 'You have no right to ask such a thing.'

'We will discuss the exact scope of my rights where you are concerned at a more convenient time,' he said icily. 'You are my future wife, and you will wear my ring.'

'But it's sheer hypocrisy,' she protested miserably. 'We don't have that kind of relationship. This ring's a—a love token.'

He stifled a curse. 'Is this what you want?' he demanded violently. Before she could move or say anything, he had gone on one knee at her side. She shrank back on the settle, a sudden wave of heat sweeping over her body at his sudden proximity. Before she could guess what he intended to do, he took her hand. For a moment, he stared down at the slenderness of the fingers in his own, and then he turned it over and carried it to his lips. His mouth moved warm and sensuous across her palm, and a long, sweet shiver ran through her body. His lips moved lazily to her upturned wrist and she tensed, miserably sure he would sense the utter tumult in her pulses. She closed her eyes, desperately seeking to hide the revelations she feared they might contain, and felt the smooth chill of the great ring as it slid on to her finger.

She sensed that he had moved from her side, and clasped her hands tightly together in her lap, concealing the ring.

When she did venture to look up, he was standing, one arm resting on the mantelpiece as he had been when she had first seen him. The bitter brooding look was back in his face.

'I hope that fulfilled your obvious expectations,' he shot at her.

'I expected nothing.' She bent her head. 'But I suppose you can count it as another victory, *monsieur*. Now may I go?'

'*Un moment*.' He paused, then said without a trace of emotion, 'Our marriage will take place the day after tomorrow.'

Andrea felt physically sick. Nothing—not even the gift of the ring—had prepared her for this. She felt trapped.

'Does it have to be so soon?' Her voice sounded totally unreal in her own ears.

'Yes.' He pushed at the burning logs with the toe of his boot. 'My lawyers tell me that Simone is planning to start proceedings to contest Jean-Paul's will almost at once. I wish to forestall her, naturally, so there can be no further delay.'

'But there are legal formalities, surely,' she said faintly.

'All dealt with weeks ago. You have a short memory, *mademoiselle*.'

Andrea stifled a groan. Clare had kept from her the full extent of her involvement—she realised that now. But she had no time to waste in useless recriminations. The only thing she could do now was get away from this place as quickly as possible. The need to recover Clare's letter could not weigh with her now, she thought desperately.

She forced herself to think calmly. She had to make him think she was resigned to her fate.

'I wish you'd warned me earlier.' She even managed to sound a little sulky. 'I do have some shopping still to do.'

He raised his eyebrows. 'I see no problem. Gaston may drive you to Clermont-Ferrand tomorrow.'

She lowered her lashes to hide the gleam of triumph in her eyes. 'Thank you,' she acquiesced meekly.

It would mean, of course, she would have to leave behind most of the luggage she had brought with her, and take only what she could carry, but it would be worth it. Once in Clermont-Ferrand, it would surely be easy to give Gaston the slip, and find some means of returning to Paris.

She bade him a subdued goodnight and went upstairs. As she reached the first floor she hesitated, looking speculatively along the corridor to the big closed double doors. His room—which just might possibly contain Clare's letter. Common sense told her that she owed Clare nothing, but the same did not apply to her uncle and aunt. It was their heartbreak she had to consider in all this. She had to face the fact that by coming here in this deliberate deception and then running away, she might well have made things worse for Clare. Blaise Levallier would be angry when he learned the truth, and the retribution he might seek could well be swift and unpleasant for all concerned.

But if she was able to retrieve Clare's letter, then his major weapon would be lost to him.

She looked half-fearfully over her shoulder, as if expecting to see him following her up the stairs. But he had given no indication that he intended to have an early night himself. In fact, just as she had left the room, he had gone to the sideboard and taken out a bottle of whisky and a glass, as if he intended to make a night of it, she thought, her lips curling slightly. Now, if ever, was her chance.

Feeling rather ridiculous, she slipped off her shoes and trod cautiously along the passage in her stockinged feet. She twisted the handle gently, praying that the door would not be locked, and knew a swift flood of relief as it yielded under her pressure. She squeezed through the narrow opening and looked around her.

It was not the large room she had envisaged, or perhaps it just seemed smaller because the bed which dominated it was so vast. It was an immense four-poster with a canopy and dark red and gold curtains neatly looped back. She looked at it uneasily, wondering how many past generations had been born or had died in that bed. The single pillow it carried seemed forlorn somehow, but she crushed the thought down hastily.

Altogether it was a very masculine room, the furniture dark and unadorned, and uncompromisingly arranged around the walls. A faint aroma of the cigarettes he smoked still hung in the air, and the riding breeches and jacket he had worn earlier in the day were flung carelessly across a chair. Andrea eyed them disapprovingly, wondering if she dared hang them in the wardrobe where they belonged, and eventually deciding she did not. The most hopeful piece of furniture seemed to be the dressing table which was lavishly supplied with drawers. She walked over and sank down on to the dressing stool, then biting her lip, she opened the first drawer. But her hopes sank with each succeeding drawer she opened. All they contained was clothes—until she came to the shallow central drawer at the top. If this contained clothes, they must be very valuable ones, for the drawer was locked. Frustrated, she tugged at the handle, wondering if there was any way she could force it open, and then, suddenly and chillingly, she knew she was being watched.

She looked up into the mirror and her eyes met Blaise Levallier's. He was leaning casually in the open doorway, watching her across the room. Her heart came up into her throat. She let her hands drop into her lap and sat there, feeling utterly humiliated and more than a little afraid.

'I have to disappoint you, *mademoiselle*.' He did not even sound particularly surprised. 'All my personal papers are lodged with my lawyer in Clermont-Ferrand. I assume that is what you are looking for—your cousin's letter.'

For one incredulous moment she thought her ears were playing tricks. Then she saw the derisive smile playing round his mouth, and realisation burst over her.

'You know!' she whispered. 'But how?'

He strolled forward. 'I have known from the very first. Did you really think I would make enquiries into your cousin's background and not take the trouble to find out her appearance? You could not be more different.'

'But you never gave the slightest sign ...'

He shrugged. 'It amused me to find out how far you were prepared to go with your little masquerade, and exactly what you hoped to achieve by it.' He looked at her dryly. 'You should not have capitulated so readily tonight, *ma mie*. My suspicions were aroused at once.'

She pressed her hands to her burning cheeks. 'I'll leave at once,' she told him unevenly. 'Would you be kind enough to allow Gaston to drive me to Clermont-Ferrand?'

His eyebrows rose. 'At this time of night? All the shops will be shut.'

She looked at him uncomprehendingly. 'Shops?'

'You cannot have forgotten so soon,' he said. 'We are to be married the day after tomorrow.'

She sprang to her feet with a little cry. 'You're mad!'

'I am perfectly sane. Nothing has changed. I still need a wife. Your cousin Clare has decided not to fulfil her obligation to me, so I will take you instead, Andrée—that is your name, is it not?'

'Well, I won't be taken,' she said wildly.

'I think you will,' he said calmly. 'My enquiries about Clare also revealed a great deal about you. For example, I know that Clare's father regards you more in the light of a second daughter than a niece. Am I not correct?'

She made no reply and after a pause he continued. 'I think your uncle would be almost as distressed were you to become involved in a public scandal as he would have been over his own daughter. Surely you don't wish to injure his health by upsetting him?'

'There can be no scandal about me.' She lifted her head and stared at him. 'I have made you no promise, in writing or otherwise.'

'There is more than one sort of scandal, *ma mie*,' he said quite gently. 'I can think of circumstances under which even you might be quite glad to marry—even me. But that is beside the point. What I promise you is that if you do not marry me as I have arranged the day after tomorrow, I will drag your family's name through the English courts and newspapers. I have an ace in my hand, after all —Philippe. The English love such stories—what is it you call them? Tug-of-love babies?'

'Blaise, I beg you.' Her eyes swam with sudden tears. 'It would be the death of Uncle Max—the end of everything he's dreamed about.'

'The answer is in your hands, Andrée.' His face was dark and forbidding as he looked down at her. 'Do as I ask, and become my wife so that I can obtain legal custody of Philippe.' He paused. 'Once the legalities have been satisfied and Simone is no longer a threat, perhaps we can consider some alternative.'

'You'll let me go?' Her white face pleaded with him. 'You'll have the marriage annulled as soon as it's possible to do so?'

He looked at her, taking in the trembling lips and the huge tears which threatened at any moment to spill over, and his face was bleak. Then he bent his head.

'Very well, *mademoiselle*. A year of your life—possibly less—in exchange for a child's happiness. Is it a bargain?'

'A bargain,' she echoed tonelessly. Reality had receded and her mind seemed to be revolving in endless circles of aimlessness. Perhaps when she was alone she would be able to think more clearly, come to terms with this intolerable situation. She still could not believe what had happened to her in these few brief moments. A year, she whispered inwardly, he promised it would only be for a year. But at the same time she was aware of the growing conviction pressing down on her that the whole course of her life had changed. A year is a long time, a warning voice told her. Much can happen in a year. But she wouldn't think about that now.

She moved forward, catching her foot on the worn carpet and stumbling a little. He caught her arm, steadying her so that for a brief instant she leaned against him.

And reality returned with that fleeting, scorching awareness. She tore herself away from him.

'Don't touch me!' She hardly recognised her own voice.

Something came and went in the dark eyes so steadily regarding her, but his voice was calm when he spoke.

'You flatter yourself, *mademoiselle*. Believe me, if I had any urge to touch you, it would not be the kind of furtive contact that would disgrace a boy of sixteen. As it is, my sole impulse where you are concerned is to beat you soundly, and I suggest you leave now before I yield to it.'

She hesitated, her face flaming, then hastily retrieving her shoes, went to the door with as much dignity as she could muster.

Her own room seemed like a sanctuary, and she closed the door and leaned back against it with her eyes shut. What have I done? she thought frantically. Oh, God, what have I done?

CHAPTER FOUR

It hardly seemed possible that she should sleep, yet she did, overwhelmed by her body's utter weariness, and woke to find the room filled with sunshine and Madame Bresson standing over her, holding a large tray.

'Did I oversleep?' Andrea sat up unwillingly, pushing the cloud of hair back from her face. 'I'm sorry if I have caused you any trouble.'

But Madame's face was wreathed in smiles. For the bride of Monseigneur, no effort could be grudged, she assured Andrea, and her twinkling eyes suggested that Mademoiselle was wise to sleep while she could ...

In spite of her utter disinclination to face the day ahead of her, Andrea could not help enjoying the coffee and warm rolls, and it was a relief not to have to consume them downstairs under Blaise Levallier's caustic gaze. She bit her lip. She intended to keep out of his way today, even if it meant spending all her time in her room.

'Mademoiselle wishes me to run her bath?' Madame Bresson had solicitously returned. 'There is not a great deal of time.'

'Before what?' Andrea replaced her cup on the tray.

Madame looked at her as if she had lost her wits. 'Before it is time to set out for Clermont-Ferrand. Monseigneur is waiting to take you shopping.'

For a moment Andrea sat motionless, then she pushed the tray away. 'I've had enough to eat, thank you,' she said curtly. 'And I'm not going shopping. Perhaps you would tell—Monseigneur that I have a headache.'

Madame stared at her, obviously taken aback. 'But, *mademoiselle*, Monseigneur has cancelled appointments to put this day at your disposal. And Clermont-Ferrand is a fine city. You will enjoy the drive and the fresh air will cure your headache.'

'I think I know what is best for my own headache,'

Andrea said with a snap. She knew she was being childish, but it seemed unimportant compared with the prospect of a day spent with Blaise Levallier. 'You can thank Monseigneur—you can even apologise to him if it makes you feel better—but you can tell him I am not driving anywhere with him today. Besides, I've changed my mind. I don't need to do any shopping.'

Madame, her feathers obviously ruffled by this sudden intractability on the part of her future mistress, picked up the tray and made for the door, her back speaking volumes of disapproval.

Andrea turned on to her stomach and punched moodily at her pillow. Blaise knew perfectly well why she had wanted to go into Clermont-Ferrand. The only reason he persisted in referring to the trip was in order to torment her with her own helplessness. Well, he would not have the pleasure of seeing her squirm!

She folded her arms and rested her cheek on them, staring unseeingly in front of her. She would have to write to Clare now, but could her volatile cousin be relied on to accept the situation and not make exactly the sort of trouble they were trying to avoid? She would have to make it more than clear in the letter that she had agreed to this incredible marriage only for Uncle Max's sake, and that she would be free again once a year had passed. And she would also have to write to her employers, telling them that she would not be returning after her holiday. They wouldn't be very pleased, she knew, and it was unlikely that they would want her back once this period of servitude was over. She sighed, conscious of a curious feeling of desolation. It was one thing to tell herself that she had got herself into this mess with her eyes open, and quite another to come to terms with the situation. And one increasingly disturbing aspect of this was her own attraction to Blaise Levallier. It was easy enough to tell herself that she hated him, and recount the more than adequate reasons for doing so, but far less simple to dismiss the trembling awareness he aroused in her. And the prospect of spending perhaps a year living in the comparative intimacy of the same house frankly terrified her.

She gave the ring she wore a brooding glance. Almost against her will, her fingers curled sensuously into the palm of her hand as she recalled how his mouth had lingered against her flesh. But that, she thought, was something she needed to forget and quickly too if she was to have any peace of mind at all.

There was a knock at the door, and she twisted on to her side, staring at it. Surely this wasn't Madame Bresson with yet another attempt at persuasion, she thought, her mouth pursing impatiently as she called '*Entrez.*'

But it was Blaise Levallier who strode in, his tall figure taut with anger as he halted a few feet from the bed and regarded her grimly.

'For how much longer do you intend to keep me waiting, *mademoiselle*?' His tone was icy.

Andrea's poise deserted her under his piercing scrutiny and she found herself huddling the duvet up around her shoulders.

'You're free to leave whenever you wish, *monsieur*,' she replied as steadily as she was able. 'Perhaps Madame Bresson didn't give you my message . . .'

The curl of his lip showed her precisely what he thought of her message.

'You had better hurry,' he said. 'We have a long drive ahead of us before this shopping expedition can even begin.'

'I don't need to do any shopping. I thought I'd made that clear.' Andrea gave him a frustrated look. 'I have everything I need, thank you. Now if you would just get out of my room, I'd like to go back to sleep.'

He did turn on his heel, but not to leave as she had hoped. Instead he walked over to the massive wardrobe and threw open the door. The limited selection of clothes she had brought with her looked slightly pathetic hanging in its cavernous depths. He swung back to her, his face black.

'I see no wedding dress, *mademoiselle*.'

She stared at him. 'Wedding dress?' she repeated inanely.

His mouth twisted impatiently. 'Surely you don't need another reminder? We are to be married tomorrow. You need a dress to wear for the ceremony.'

'Surely that isn't necessary,' she protested. 'It isn't as if it's going to be a conventional marriage ...'

'You deceive yourself, *ma mie*.' Hands resting on his hips, he walked back to the bed and stood looking down at her. 'The performance of the ceremony will be as conventional as anyone could wish, no matter what may happen afterwards. My marriage will be an occasion in the village, and you will look the part of a happy bride if nothing else. You will be on show both at the civil ceremony in Craudon and at the religious service in the village church, and you will use your undoubted ability as an actress to play the role of the loving wife. And you will wear a white dress and a veil, because that is what people will expect of you.'

'I will not!' She glared at him, her breast heaving stormily. 'It would be total hypocrisy.'

'Why is that?' he asked contempuously. 'Is white no longer an appropriate colour for you to wear?'

'Why, you ...' Fury made her incoherent. 'Get out of my room!'

'As your fiancé, I have every right to be in your room,' he reminded her, his voice steely. 'Almost as many rights as a husband, *ma chère*. I advise you not to forget it. Now, get dressed. We have wasted enough time.'

He bent and before she could resist, pulled the concealing cover. Andrea gave a little outraged cry, hastily restoring order to the crumpled folds of her blue gingham nightdress, but he seemed totally uninterested in her state of *déshabille*. He was back at the wardrobe, pulling her cream linen suit from its hanger, and rooting through the drawers of her dressing table for a handful of filmy underwear which he tossed unceremoniously on to the bed beside her.

He glanced at his watch. 'You have five minutes, *mademoiselle*. If you have not joined me downstairs by that time,

I shall dress you myself, so do not pretend I have not warned you.'

For a moment after the door closed behind him, Andrea lay quite still, seething with temper. Then almost frantically she realised that she was just wasting precious seconds. She had no doubt at all that he would return as he had threatened, and she scrambled off the bed, rushing to the washstand and splashing herself hastily with the lukewarm water the jug contained.

She had just fastened the last button on her jacket, and was knotting a long silk scarf around her throat, when the door opened and Blaise came back into the room without the courtesy this time of a preliminary knock.

He was still frowning, she saw as their eyes met in the mirror, but he gave a faint nod as if her appearance satisfied him.

'You are ready?'

'I have my hair to do.' She hated the tremor in her voice and hoped he had not noticed.

He came and stood behind her, so close to her that she could feel the warmth from his body.

'Leave it loose,' he advised quietly. He reached past her and picked up her hairbrush from the dressing table. She tensed, clinging to the edge of the dressing table as he began to draw the brush gently at first and then with increasing vigour through her tangled hair. He lifted the soft chestnut strands away from the nape of her neck, and let them fall slowly back into place. A quiver of almost unbearable sensation ran through her, and her mouth went dry. For a brief instant she imagined leaning back against him and feeling his arms close round her, his hands sliding up under the loose jacket to find her breasts. She closed her eyes involuntarily, overwhelmed by the force of her emotions, bewildered by the potency of her own desire.

When she opened them again she found she was staring straight into his in the mirror. The dark depths of his gaze held her mesmerically. He seemed to be asking her a question to which her body had an only too compelling answer.

She swallowed and reached for her handbag with hands that shook.

'Shall—shall we go?'

'As you wish.' His face and voice were enigmatic alike. He tossed the hairbrush almost carelessly back on to the dressing table and stood aside to allow her to precede him out of the room. For a moment she was afraid that her shaking legs would not obey her, then she squared her shoulders and lifted her chin and made herself walk past him with an assumption of calm.

It did not last her long, however. When they emerged into the courtyard and she saw that the vehicle awaiting them was the hired car she had driven there from Paris, the breath left her body in one strangled gasp.

'If you had only known it was still here, eh?' Blaise's voice held an element of lazy amusement, and she cast him one fulminating look before climbing into the passenger seat.

He drove well. She grudgingly had to admit that, as he negotiated with ease the twisting road which had brought her heart into her mouth, and under different circumstances she could have enjoyed this chance to really look at the spectacular scenery around them.

As it was, she sat, her hands stiffly clenched in her lap with temper, staring woodenly ahead of her through the windscreen as if she had been blinkered. She had made up her mind to receive any attempts he made at conversation in stony silence, and it was as if he could read her mind, because he said nothing.

Gradually and in spite of herself, the sheer exuberant beauty of the autumn day began to get through to her and she began almost insensibly to relax, leaning back in her seat and enjoying the warmth of the sun on her face and neck. After a while, she stole a sideways look at her companion. Surely he could not intend to drive all the way to Clermont-Ferrand without uttering a word? she thought with a twist of the lips at her own lack of resolution.

From where she sat, the scarred side of his face was hidden from her, and she could not suppress a pang of regret as her eyes travelled over the proud clean lines of cheekbone, nose and mouth. She had imagined his attention was wholly concentrated on the road ahead, and it was a shock when she saw his mouth draw into the bitter lines she had come to dread.

'What are you staring at, *mademoiselle*? Are you asking yourself why I don't make use of plastic surgery to render myself less unsightly?'

'Nothing was further from my mind,' she denied hastily. 'But as you've brought the subject up, haven't you ever considered doing so?'

'No. My lack of attraction is of no concern to me. Besides, my scars are—useful. They serve as a constant reminder.'

'Of what?' she asked rather faintly.

'Of the fact that nothing lasts, *ma mie*. And that emotions, particularly that strange involvement we call love, are the most ephemeral of all.'

'That's a very cynical point of view.'

'It's a lesson I have been taught by life,' he retorted. He did not volunteer any more information and Andrea sat staring ahead of her through the windscreen, trying to resolve her confused thoughts. She knew that his bitter words must be referring to his broken engagement. Yet because one woman had shown the selfishness and triviality of her nature, were they all to be condemned? He must have loved her very much, she thought, for her to have affected him so deeply, and she was shocked at the pain her musings cost her. What was she thinking of? she wondered frantically. Whatever happened, she could not get involved emotionally with this man. There was no future in it, she told herself vehemently, apart from the fact that her pride should safeguard her from any warmth in her feelings towards this man who was trapping her into this empty marriage. She needed to hate him. Indifference would not be enough, she knew instinctively.

But he was so wrong to imagine his damaged face had in any way detracted from his physical attraction, she thought achingly. The sensual power he could exert terrified her and enthralled her at the same time, and she was bewildered at the potential force of her own response to him.

Besides, his visible scars were negligible compared with the emotional damage he had suffered. It was daunting to imagine how much love and generosity would be needed before that was healed. One thing was certain—before it happened, she would be long gone. It was a thought which depressed her in spite of her attempts to lash herself into resentment against him by reminding herself that until then she would be little better than a prisoner in his house. And it occurred to her starkly that no matter how far she might go, she would never truly be free again.

She shook herself mentally, fighting the realisation down. This was dangerous ground, where she could not venture. Must not, if she was to retain even a vestige of her peace of mind in the days ahead of her.

Blaise parked the car in a quiet side-street, and they walked to the Rue du Port, where the main shops were situated. Andrea would like to have lingered outside some of the antique shops they passed on the way, but Blaise seemed to have retired to some remote interior fastness and showed no disposition to indulge her. As it was, she was almost obliged to trot to keep up with his long stride, and she was breathless by the time they reached the shop of his choice. She raised her eyebrows a little, imagining that he would have picked a large store rather than this cramped-looking boutique displaying a scarf and an artificial rose in its small window, but when they got inside she realised he knew what he was about. The proprietress herself came forward to serve them, a sophisticated woman in her forties with deceptively sleepy eyes.

Blaise and she indulged in a murmured conversation from which Andrea found herself excluded, to her annoyance. They were obviously talking about her, she fumed inwardly, so they might have had the decency to let her know what was being said.

At last the woman turned to her, favouring her with a

speculative look which Andrea knew had assessed her figure down to the last centimetre. 'If Mademoiselle would come with me?'

She had no choice but to comply. She was shown into a spacious fitting room, with mirrors on all sides, and an assistant came in carrying several tissue-swathed white dresses over her arm.

Andrea decided the time had come to make a stand. 'Not white,' she said firmly, indicating the dresses. She was not going to allow herself to be adorned like the traditional virgin sacrifice, she thought angrily, for a crowd of strangers to snigger over. She was not a doll without feelings. A white wedding encompassed a whole range of emotions and meanings that had no place at all in her relationship with Blaise.

If she had only had the assistant to deal with, she might have got away with it. But she had not reckoned with Madame. Her smile might be charming, but it was quite implacable, and Andrea found her suit had been removed and hung tenderly on a hanger and herself zipped into the first of the white dresses without quite knowing how it had happened.

'*Non*,' she said forcibly to a variety of Andreas, formal in white satin.

To her surprise Madame was in total and amiable agreement with her, but it was only a temporary respite. The dress was not suitable, but there were plenty more, and now the assistant had been despatched to fetch some veils, 'so that Mademoiselle could behold the full effect.'

Eventually, '*Regardez*,' Madame urged fondly, and Andrea found herself staring incredulously at a stranger, slim and ethereal in a cloud of silk organza, the floating skirt misted with embroidered flowers.

Madame clucked round her, arranging the veil with satisfied twitches, and then before Andrea could do anything, she had swept back the curtain and ushered her out into the main showroom where Blaise was waiting.

She thought wildly, 'It's unlucky for him to see me like

this—unlucky,' before common sense reminded her that none of the sweet traditions of marriage could have any meaning for them. His eyes as he looked at her were cold, his dark brows drawn together in an impatient frown. He didn't like the dress, she told herself. Now he must see how ridiculous this whole charade was. Perhaps he was remembering that other girl whose wedding gown might also have been chosen, and who might have paraded for him, wearing it and demanding that he admire her beauty.

He looked over her head at Madame standing behind and gave a barely perceptible nod. '*Ravissante,*' he said dryly. 'You can supply Mademoiselle with everything else she needs—shoes, for example?'

Andrea went to him across the carpet, the dress rustling softly. She laid her hand appealingly on his arm.

'Blaise, please listen to me. I can't wear this dress.'

'Why not?' He looked her over with the impersonality he would have devoted to a dummy in a shop window. 'It seems to fit you admirably.'

'It isn't a question of the fit.' She knew Madame was watching them curiously, and lowered her voice even further. 'It—it just wouldn't be right. Surely you can see that.'

It was a romantic gown—a gown for a happy girl to wear for her lover. It had nothing to do with the cold, transient relationship she was entering into.

He raised his eyebrows. 'I think it is entirely suitable. Tomorrow you will look as the world expects you to look. Don't look so anguished, *ma mie*. Regard it as a costume for a carnival that you wear for a few hours and then discard for ever.'

There was no way that she could convince him that this was a betrayal of all this lovely dress was meant to represent. He would simply accuse her of being over-emotional, and he could be right. Why couldn't she regard it all as he did, as a masquerade in which she was required to act a role for a few hours? Why couldn't she crush this growing conviction that it wasn't going to be as simple as all that?

When the striped white and silver boxes had been bestowed in the car. Blaise suggested abruptly that they should do some sightseeing. They saw the Place Delille with its charming fountain, where Peter the Hermit preached the First Crusade, and the great black Gothic cathedral towering over the older part of the city. Andrea found it spectacular but oddly oppressive, though this might have been attributable to her emotional state. They had lunch at Royat, on the terrace overlooking the central gardens, and she was glad to be able to relax, and enjoy the sunshine and the wine. Royat had been a fashionable spa in the nineteenth century, and gazing up at the elaborate façades of the hotels, Andrea thought it would not be difficult to imagine the Empress Eugénie with crinoline and parasol descending the steps, acknowledging the bows of the crowd. She smiled at her own fancifulness.

'What amuses you?' Blaise was lounging back in his chair, his eyes narrowed slightly against the sun.

'It doesn't matter,' she said hurriedly, slightly ashamed of allowing her thoughts to wander on such trivial lines. Anyone would think she didn't have a care in the world.

'As you wish,' he shrugged, his lips tightening fractionally.

She wished then that she had told him. Relations were sufficiently strained between them now without him believing she was deliberately keeping things from him. She gave an inward sigh. Even when they had been looking round the cathedral, conversation between them had been kept to a minimum and restricted to purely impersonal subjects. How long did he intend this to go on? Had he no intention of talking about themselves—their future, or did he merely expect the marriage to proceed the following day without any further discussion? It seemed frankly incredible. She stole a sideways glance at him. He was smoking a cigarette and watching the blue smoke curl into the air, as if it were his only concern.

Although it was late in the season, the terrace was busy, and Andrea found herself at first idly and then more intently assessing her chances of losing herself among the chattering groups. Blaise had not yet paid for their lunch. This could delay him for a few minutes, so if she made the excuse that she needed to find a public convenience ... A sudden feeling of excitement possessed her. She would go to one of the hotels and book a room. He would be unlikely to look for her there. He would imagine that she would want to get out of Clermont-Ferrand as fast as possible.

She saw that he was looking round for the waiter and rose with a slight yawn.

'Will you excuse me for a moment?' she said.

'Of course.' He rose with her, picking her handbag up from the table and passing it to her. His voice was cool and courteous. 'In case you should be thinking foolish thoughts, *ma mie*, I should perhaps warn you that I took the precaution of abstracting your passport from your bag while you were trying on dresses.'

It took a monumental effort to conceal her chagrin. She said coolly, 'Quite unnecessary, *monsieur*. I am resigned to my fate.'

'I hope you are.' His face was unsmiling. 'Perhaps it will not be the ordeal you imagine.'

Suddenly she was angry, and desperation lent an added bite to her words.

'And what ordeal do you fear, Blaise? Being jilted a second time?'

He was very pale beneath his tan, but she went on relentlessly, 'Does it make you proud, *monsieur*, to know that the only way you can persuade a girl to marry you is by blackmail—by threatening to destroy the people she loves. Will it do your family credit, do you suppose?'

'What are you hoping for?' he asked between his teeth. 'That I'll throw you your passport and tell you to go to hell out of my sight? If so, then I have to disappoint you, *mademoiselle*. Once you're my wife it will be my pleasure to teach you some manners.'

Andrea's cheeks were flaming, and she was acutely conscious of the curious glances being cast at them from neighbouring tables.

'Can't we go on with this discussion somewhere less

public?' she appealed in a low voice.

'There is nothing more to discuss.' A flick of his fingers summoned the waiter, and the bill was paid. Then they were moving off, his hand gripping her arm.

'You're hurting me,' she protested, trying to pull free.

'I wish it was your neck,' he said grimly, and she flinched at his tone.

'So do I.' Sheer bravado drove her on. 'At least then I'd be rid of you!'

They were in the shadow of a tall hedge. He turned suddenly, pushing her against it so violently that she felt twigs snapping against her back, and the scrape of stems and dried leaves through the material of her suit.

'I said I'd teach you manners when we were married.' He grated the words at her. 'I see the first lesson must start now.'

He took her by the shoulders, jerking her towards him so hard that the protest she was going to make was choked off in her throat. Then his mouth came down on hers, and all protest was useless.

When at last he let her go she was trembling so much that she felt she wanted to faint, or be sick. She had been kissed by him in mockery. Now she had been kissed in anger, if one could call that brutal, unrelenting assault on her mouth a kiss. If he wanted her to feel degraded, then he had succeeded, she thought, lifting her hand instinctively to her bruised and swollen lips. And the worst of it was she knew that if she had sensed the slightest glimmer of genuine passion from him, as opposed to violent anger, then she would not have been able to stop herself from responding to it. The briefest sign from him that this was not solely punishment, and her lips would have parted for him voluntarily.

'When you're ready, *mademoiselle*. Gaston will be waiting for us.' With insulting casualness, he brushed some leaves from her hair, his fingers tightening round one silken chestnut strand until she was forced to look up at him. His voice roughened. 'Don't provoke me again, Andrée.'

He took her arm and began to walk her along the path again.

When they arrived back where the car was parked, Gaston was waiting with a Land-Rover. Andrea stood in silence while the dress boxes were transferred from one vehicle to the other, and then she climbed into the passenger seat beside Gaston while Blaise drove the hired car back to the garage it had come from. She was glad of Gaston's phlegmatic company. If he noticed her bruised mouth and generally dishevelled appearance, he gave no sign, seeming content to whistle unrecognisable tunes through a gap in his front teeth.

The return journey to the chateau was quite a different matter. Andrea was obliged to sit squashed between the two men while Blaise drove, and she was acutely conscious of his proximity. What desultory conversation there was related solely to farming matters, and was conducted in French across the top of her head—as if she was a bale of hay, she thought indignantly, flexing her shoulder muscles.

She was cramped and uncomfortable when the Land-Rover finally came to rest in the courtyard, and she climbed down stiffly ignoring Blaise's hand outstretched to assist her.

'Do you wish Gaston to carry your purchases up to your room?' He detained her peremptorily.

It would have given her the utmost pleasure to tell him precisely what he could do with all of them, but she did not dare risk another explosion of his wrath, so she thanked him coldly and walked on ahead.

She found Madame Bresson in the kitchen looking harassed. She had been cleaning a mound of silver, and washing glasses she had unearthed from one of the large cupboards, and Andrea realised with a shock of dismay that these preparations must be for the guests who would presumably be returning to the chateau after the wedding for some kind of reception. She had imagined the whole affair would be so much more private, and she tried rather stumblingly to explain this to Madame Bresson. But

Madame obviously did not comprehend, and began to reassure Andrea, under the apparent impression that she was simply suffering from bridal nerves. Andrea excused herself at last, claiming that her day in Clermont had exhausted her, which was not so very far from the truth, and that she would forgo dinner, and have an early night instead. She had half expected Madame Bresson to protest, but the housekeeper obviously saw nothing strange in her decision.

The boxes containing her dress and veil and other things were piled neatly on the bed, and Andrea surveyed them moodily as she kicked off her shoes. Much as she wanted to ignore them, she knew she would have to take that lovely gown out of its wrappings and hang it up. It didn't deserve to spend a night in creases. She put it away in the wardrobe on a padded hanger, and laid the coronet and veil along her dressing table, glancing at herself with sudden self-criticism in the mirror as she did so. A light make-up would suffice, she thought, and she would put her hair up under the coronet. A quick pang of regret smote her. On the rare occasions when she had imagined her own wedding, it had always been with her family there—Clare to act as bridesmaid, and Aunt Marian to advise her on colour schemes and hairstyles. She had never envisaged that she would be totally alone like this. Her throat was aching suddenly and her eyes stung, and throwing herself across the bed, she gave way to a fit of desolate weeping.

When it was over she lay for a long time, the damp ball of her handkerchief pressed against her mouth, and tried soberly to face the facts. The trouble she was in she had brought upon herself. Tomorrow she was to be married to a man who had demonstrated his utter indifference to her as a woman, and had made it plain she was merely being used by him. Unfortunately, and she resolutely smothered a little choking sob, she did not echo his indifference. It was ironic to think how she had always despised women who were ruled by their senses and emotions, and now she was one of them, as vulnerable as any. One essential was to keep this vulnerability from Blaise. He must never know the aching, trembling need he could rouse in her almost at his lightest touch, or his total cynicism might prompt him to take advantage of the fact that she was there, his wife and available. A union like that, she thought, simply fulfilling a physical need, would be the ultimate in degradation. All she could do was keep out of his way as much as possible and avoid provoking him as she had done today when she was forced to be in his company.

She was half-dozing through sheer emotional weariness when she heard the knock on the door. She didn't reply. It was bound to be Madame Bresson coming to persuade her to have some dinner, and if she kept quite still, Madame would, with luck, assume she was asleep and go away again. She bit her lip with irritation when she heard the door open quietly and someone enter the room. Then her body went rigid as she realised that the step she could hear approaching was certainly not Madame's. She made herself lie still, and breathe slowly and deeply, thankful that her back was turned away from the door.

It was torture, lying there in the still room, knowing that he was standing looking down at her and waiting for him to say something. She tried to control a nervous swallow, afraid that he would guess she was only counterfeiting sleep. After what seemed an eternity, he turned away and she heard the door close, equally softly. It was a long time before she dared turn around. She had the absurd impression that he might be still there, waiting for her to reveal the fact that she was awake and aware of his presence, but the room was empty in the evening shadows. She sat up with a little shiver. She would be more comfortable if she undressed and got under the covers. She put out her hand listlessly for her folded nightdress and paused. There was another package lying on the bed.

Andrea was bewildered. For a moment she wondered if she had simply overlooked one of the packages Gaston had brought upstairs, but a moment's rational thought convinced her that this could not be the case and that she had unpacked all the things she had chosen in Clermont and put them away. So what was this?

She picked it up. It was a flat parcel, and very light, tied elegantly with ribbons. Was this why Blaise had entered her room so quietly, to leave this on the bed beside her? It seemed incredible and totally out of character. But then what did she really know about his character anyway? she asked herself, recalling the bruising pressure of his mouth on hers in the gardens at Royat.

At last she could not restrain her curiosity any further and she untied the ribbons and unfolded the paper wrappings. Her hands seemed suddenly full of filmy lace, and as she turned wonderingly towards the window, she realised with an indrawn breath that what she was holding was a nightgown, white and sheer as gossamer with slender ribbon shoulder straps, and a matching ribbon drawstring giving Empire line emphasis to the bustline. For a moment she stared down at it unbelievingly, then with burning cheeks she thrust it back into its wrappings.

What did he mean by buying her so intimate a gift? she asked herself, dry-mouthed at the implications which presented themselves. How did this transparent piece of enticement fit in with the business arrangement he had promised her? Oh God, what was she getting herself into with this marriage? Just as she thought she had got it all sorted out in her own mind, he had come and upset all her preconceptions and decisions. She was a prey once more to all her earlier doubts and misgivings. Was this gift an unequivocal warning that she could not rely on his previous undertaking to forgo his marital rights? And how would her own strength of will withstand such an onslaught?

For a shattering moment, her too-vivid imagination made her feel what it would be like to be in Blaise's arms, with only that fragile white cloud as the sole tantalising barrier between them ... She shook her head violently, pressing her hands against her eyes to dispel the image, digging her nails into her flesh so that pain would replace the other, pleasurable sensations she had to ignore.

And ignore them she must, if she was to emerge from this affair with her self-respect. He must be made to see that his usage of her was to be restricted to the cold legalities of their original arrangement. She would not be seduced by his gifts or forced into submission by the brutality of his kisses.

She swung herself off the bed and walked to the door, carrying the parcel containing the nightgown. She was counting on the fact that he would be downstairs and that his room would be deserted, and her instinct was right. She shook the nightdress free of its wrappings, and not without a pang of regret for the lovely thing it was, tore it from neckline to hem until it was in rags. Then she threw the remnants across his bed and ran back to her own room as if she was being hunted by the devil.

CHAPTER FIVE

ANDREA put down her untouched glass of champagne and wandered over to the window. The sky had been overcast and threatening all day, and now that threat was being fulfilled in long silver spears of rain, dashing themselves against the ancient panes. She leaned her forehead thankfully against the cool glass. The pins which Madame Bresson had lent her to secure her coiffure seemed individually and collectively intent on impaling her scalp, and the weight of the veil was dragging at her neck.

She was alone, for the first time that day it seemed. Blaise had gone out into the hall to bid goodbye to Monsieur le Curé, and the local doctor who had lingered behind after the other guests who had come back to drink their health at the chateau had departed.

Andrea had smiled and murmured thanks for their rather boisterous congratulations until she thought her face would break in half with the effort of it all.

She heard the heavy outer door close, and swung round waiting for Blaise to reappear. In the formality of a dark suit and white shirt he seemed even taller and infinitely less approachable than he had ever been. A silence seemed to hang between them, heavy and brooding.

Andrea cleared her throat. 'Have—have they gone?'

'Yes.' He raised his brows interrogatively. 'Why do you ask? Are you so anxious to be alone with me?'

She felt the colour creeping into her cheeks, and sought to mask her embarrassment. 'That's hardly likely, is it?' she said, her tone deliberately insolent.

His eyes narrowed slightly. 'Have a care,' he warned her, and she felt her stomach muscles contract nervously.

There had been no opportunity for private conversation between them up to now, so she had no idea what his reaction had been to her destruction of his gift the previous night. But at the same time as she had stood at his side at the Mairie and later in the small parish church of St Jean des Roches, she had been nervously aware of—something—some kind of strong emotion only barely held in check. Outwardly there was no glimpse of it. His eyes when they met hers were veiled, and when he had bent to claim the traditional bridal kiss after the Curé had pronounced them man and wife, his lips had barely grazed her cheek.

These signs of indifference should have been reassuring, but she did not feel consoled in the slightest. She now regretted her hasty action from the bottom of her heart. It would have been far better to have put the nightdress away in a drawer and pretend it did not exist. She realised that now—now that it was too late. And she could not even apologise about it, without revealing the importance the incident had assumed in her mind. All she could do was ignore the whole thing, and hope that he would do the same.

Her head was really aching now, and in an effort to relieve her tension she unfastened her coronet and veil and took them off, pulling the remaining pins from her hair and letting it tumble round her face.

She thought she heard a muffled sound from Blaise, and

her eyes flew, startled, to his face. But she must have been mistaken, for he was quite impassive, reaching into his pocket for a cigarette and lighting it. She moistened her lips.

'Is it all right if I change now? We—we shan't have any more visitors today, shall we?'

His mouth twisted derisively. 'I imagine not. Our—privacy will be respected, for what it is worth.' He looked her over. 'Why are you in such a hurry to change? You look very beautiful as you are.'

She swallowed. 'I'd be more—comfortable in something else,' she said awkwardly. 'There's no reason for me to go on wearing this dress. I've done as you asked—played the part to the best of my ability. Now I'd like to be myself again, that's all.'

'And what is this self you are so anxious to recapture?' He blew a reflective smoke ring. 'You are now Madame Blaise Levallier, *ma mie*. Perhaps you should remember that.'

'I'm not likely to forget it,' she muttered, her eyes drawn unwillingly to the wide gold wedding ring he had placed on her finger only a few hours before. She lifted her hand. 'I have a constant reminder.'

'But hardly a permanent one.' He took off his jacket and draped it carelessly over the back of one of the dining chairs. 'Perhaps I shall think of a way to make your new identity more real to you, *madame*.'

She was instantly wary, but she forced her voice to normality, disguising her nervousness. 'I've thought of one already.'

'Indeed?' His smile mocked her. 'You fascinate me, *ma chère*.'

'I know our marriage is only a nominal one,' she went on steadily. 'But does this also apply to my position in the household?'

'What are you talking about?'

'Madame Bresson told me that she hoped to have some time to devote to—other things, once we were married,' she said. 'Is this your intention? Am I going to have any real authority here?'

His face was enigmatic. 'What authority do you wish?' he drawled.

'There are a lot of changes that could be made to the benefit of the chateau,' she said. 'I'd like to try and make our living quarters a little less stark, for one thing. I have some money of my own,' she added defensively. 'Can I have a free hand or do I have to refer everything to you first?'

'I should have to sanction any major items of expenditure,' he said. 'I prefer that you do not use your money for this purpose. I am not yet totally poverty-stricken, you know.'

'I didn't imagine you were.' She bit her lip. 'I—I'd like to help, though.'

'I am not rejecting your assistance—just requesting that you confine it to practical matters.' He walked over to her and put a hand under her chin, smiling faintly at the rebellion in her face. 'If you wish, you could begin by preparing a room for Philippe. Now that we are married, my lawyer will be communicating with Simone, informing her that his custody should be transferred to me. He may be joining us very soon.'

'I see. How old is Philippe?'

'He will soon be five.' He was silent for a moment. 'It does not disturb you—having to assume responsibility for a child you have never met?'

'I like children,' she replied unthinkingly, and coloured furiously at the amusement in his eyes.

'I shall have to bear that in mind,' he told her smoothly, and she glared at him impotently, jerking her chin free of his hand.

'Now may I go and change?'

'If you must.' He shrugged rather wryly. 'I warn you, Clothilde will be scandalised. She already disapproves because I would not allow her to put your clothes in my room while we were at church. I mention it merely because she comes from a robust generation and may decide to give you a motherly lecture on your duties as a wife.'

'Oh.' She looked away, embarrassed. 'What did you tell her?'

'Are you sure you want to hear? You might not be very pleased.'

'Indeed!' She guessed indignantly that he had insinuated she was frigid, or something equally unflattering. She heard him laugh softly as she swept past him to the door.

Safe in her room, she discarded her wedding dress with a feeling of relief. It was too delicate and fragile, and made her feel utterly vulnerable. Jeans and a sweater were an altogether safer proposition, she thought optimistically, but once she had changed she was not so sure. She studied her reflection with a frown, noticing how well the denim pants fitted her, outlining her hips and thighs. She had never in her life felt as self-conscious about her body as she did now, she thought rebelliously, crossing her arms across her breasts. It was ridiculous to start gauging the possible effect of every garment she put on like this. Nor had it ever been necessary—until now.

She picked up her hairbrush, dragging it ruthlessly through the remaining tangles. With her hair curving softly on to her shoulders, and a trace of blusher to disguise the unnatural pallor of her cheeks, she looked almost herself again.

Blaise was nowhere to be seen when she went downstairs. Doubtless he too had gone to change, and catch up on his day's work. Apart from the litter of plates and glasses in the dining room, there was nothing to suggest that this was different from any other day. Her wedding day, such as it was, was over, she thought, and crushed down the inevitable realisation that her wedding night was still to come...

She began to tidy the dining room, looking round her speculatively as she did so. It was the room they used the most, so it seemed sensible to make a start there, she thought, viewing the faded folds of the heavy brocade curtains at the windows with a disparaging eye. They had been a rich gold colour once. She knew that because she had unpicked part of the hem to check on the original colour, and she felt they must have looked most attractive against the dark panelling. The cost of similar brocade today would probably be prohibitive, but she thought she might be able to obtain the colour in a different material, using any that remained to cover some cushions for the settle. The furniture must obviously stay as it was. She was no expert, but she was sure most of the items were antiques. The carpet too had once been a glorious affair, but it was now worn to a neutral brown colour. Andrea thought it might be better to discard the carpet altogether, and dress up the flagged floor with rugs.

She carried some of the used glasses through to the kitchen, where Madame Bresson was washing up between intervals of preparing the evening meal.

Her eyes went over Andrea rather reproachfully, but she said nothing, only agreeing with enthusiasm when Andrea announced that she was about to organise the sleeping quarters for Philippe. Hastily drying her hands, she offered to accompany Andrea upstairs to look over the available bedrooms.

Before they had seen half of what was there, Andrea had realised resignedly she had taken on quite a task. Most of the rooms were large, and filled with massive, old-fashioned furniture. Not at all the environment she would have chosen for a five-year-old, she thought worriedly.

She voiced her anxieties to Madame Bresson, who clearly did not comprehend what she was getting at. In Madame's eyes, any of the chateau's rooms were more than worthy to accommodate M'sieur Philippe. She could not see that the gloomy hangings and dark forbidding furniture were any drawback at all.

'Oh, lord!' Andrea pushed her hair back irritably when the tour of inspection was over. 'These rooms are all huge. Surely there must be a smaller one somewhere?'

She looked at the last one they had visited with a jaundiced eye. Any five-year-old would feel totally lost in the depths of that massive bed.

She turned to Madame. 'Isn't there anywhere else?'

Madame spread her hands. The rooms on the floor above were unusable, she pointed out. They had been attics for many years and were even larger than the bedrooms she had seen.

Andrea bit her lip exasperatedly, then sudden inspiration came to her. She swung to Madame. 'What about the tower?'

Madame shook her head. 'No one has been in there since the death of the old Monseigneur,' she insisted. 'It is said it is not safe.'

'I think we'll take a look just the same,' Andrea said determinedly.

The doors that gave admittance to this part of the chateau were all locked and it took a prolonged search to find the keys. Andrea felt a sense of odd excitement as the heavy door on the ground floor swung back, and she stepped inside. The room she entered was crowded with furniture. Everything that had been broken or discarded from the chateau for the past hundred years seemed to have found its way there, she thought, looking round, her nose wrinkling with distaste. It was dirty and gloomy and would need a lot of work to restore it to order. But wasn't a lot of work just what she wanted? She sniffed experimentally, but although the air smelled musty she could not detect any telltale odours of rot or damp. She made towards the steep flight of stairs that led upwards in a sharp spiral, emerging through a sort of open trapdoor in the room above. This had escaped the jumble that had accumulated below and was also bare. Andrea moved out tentatively across the floorboards, testing each step she took. But the floor seemed as solid as the day it had been constructed and even suffered her jumping up and down on it without any signs of stress. She looked round her with a feeling of optimism. A child, she thought, could be happy here in this odd-shaped room with its curving walls. These had been roughly plastered, and were grimy and discoloured, but nothing, she felt, that a coat of paint couldn't improve. The furniture should be kept light and simple, she decided—perhaps just a small divan bed and a chest of drawers for clothes. If the downstairs room was cleared out and painted up, it could make a playroom, she thought, mentally adding gay curtains and warm washable rugs for the floor.

Madame Bresson's head poked rather apprehensively up through the trap. 'Take care, *madame*!'

'It's quite-safe,' Andrea assured her. 'And it will be ideal for little Philippe, don't you think?'

But Madame was frowning as she looked around, and Andrea stared as she saw her make a furtive sign of the cross.

'What's the matter?' she asked rather irritably. 'You're surely not going to tell me that the tower is haunted or something?'

Madame shook her head, but the uneasy expression did not lift from her face.

'The spirits of the dead rest in peace at Levallier, madame, may *le bon dieu* be praised. But there are still stories.'

'About this tower?' Andrea said disbelievingly. 'Now, if there had been stories about any of those gloomy bedrooms, I could have believed it.'

But Madame did not share her amusement. 'There have been tragedies, *madame*.'

'Every old house must have its share of them,' Andrea pointed out gently. 'And people have been happy here as well, so perhaps one thing cancels out the other.'

Madame sniffed, obviously unconvinced.

Andrea walked across to the window recess and stared out through the grimy panes. If the ledge was cushioned, she thought, it would make a wonderful window-seat, and the view looked down over the village, and the gleam of the distant river. In many ways she wished she was fitting out these rooms to occupy them herself, but she knew Blaise would not allow her to move so obviously out of the main part of the building.

'Madame,' the housekeeper sounded really anxious, 'before you decide, will you not consult Monseigneur?'

Andrea turned and stared at her. 'I'll mention it to him, naturally. But I can't imagine he'll object. This is an altogether cosier proposition than any of the bedrooms in the chateau. And I think the novelty of the shape will appeal to a child.'

She turned back to the window and began to wrestle with the catch that fastened the narrow casement. It was old and stiff, covered in rust, and Andrea was afraid if she forced it too much it might break off altogether, but eventually it gave way and the window swung open with a protesting squeal of disused hinges.

She gave the housekeeper a triumphant smile. 'That's all this place needs,' she announced. 'Some fresh air. The wind of change.'

She rubbed her dirty fingers of her handkerchief, then gave a slight jump as a loud whistle sounded from the courtyard below. She glanced down and saw Alan staring up at her.

'What are you doing up there?' he called. 'Playing Rapunzel?'

'Something like that,' she laughed. 'What a pity I haven't any hair to let down.'

'I think stairs would probably be less painful. Are there any? Can I come up?'

Behind her, Andrea heard Madame Bresson give a small dry cough of disapproval and guessed she felt this was an unseemly exchange for a bride to take part in on her wedding day.

'It's all a bit complicated,' she returned. 'Wait there and I'll come down.'

She went carefully down the stairs, spreading her hand on the stone wall to balance herself, and saw the pale glimmer of her wedding ring. She grimaced slightly. She had some explaining to do to Alan. Only forty-eight hours before she had been convincing him that her relationship with Blaise was purely on a business level. Now she was married to him.

She went back into the main building, leaving Madame

Bresson to lock up behind her, and emerged into the courtyard where Alan was waiting. It had stopped raining, but the air was still and chilly, and she shivered a little, wrapping her arms across her.

'Want some tea?' He looked at her hopefully.

'No, thanks.' She smiled at him, robbing her refusal of any offence. It was probably just as well to be direct, she thought. 'I'm too full of champagne and other delights.'

'Champagne?' he said uncertainly. 'Has there been a party?'

'In a way.' She removed her hand from the pocket of her jeans and held it out.

'Good God,' he said blankly. He took off his glasses and polished them carefully on a fold of his disreputable sweater. 'When did this happen?'

'Today. This morning, to be precise.' Her voice was brittle. 'You must think it very strange ...'

'It's really got nothing to do with me,' he said politely. Too politely.

'Oh, hell!' Andrea caught his arm as he turned away. 'Is the offer of tea still open? I really would like to explain.'

His hesitation was only momentary. 'Yes, of course. But there's no need to explain. God, it's your life after all. It's just that—you and the Dark Lord—I can't picture it somehow.' He flushed slightly. 'I suppose I shouldn't call Monsieur Levallier that to you either, but it just seems appropriate.'

'Yes.' She pushed her hands into her jeans pocket and began to walk slowly with him across the courtyard.

'This is all right, is it?' Alan asked suddenly when they were ensconced in his room, steaming mugs in their hands. 'It's only just occurred to me that officially you're on your honeymoon. I'm amazed he even lets you out of his sight for a minute.'

She gave a constrained smile. 'I wasn't joking when I said I was here on business,' she said after a minute. 'There—there's no romance involved. You aren't intruding on—an idyll.'

She had not realised until then what pain that spoken acknowledgment of the situation would cost her. She took a quick sip of her tea, finding an odd comfort in the scalding liquid.

'Well, I'm not even going to pretend I understand.' Alan stirred at his own brew with a pencil. He gave her a faint grin. 'I'm just checking up, you know. Making sure that no irate bridegroom is going to burst in here and cut me down. Is the *crime passionel* still a defence in France, do you know?'

She smiled and shook her head, without speaking. It was peaceful here in the gatehouse, she thought, and she would have to be careful not to start using it—and Alan—as a refuge. There were inherent dangers in this, which she could already see plainly. Alan obviously found her attractive, and it would not be fair on him to spend too much time in his company and let him draw assumptions from this that would be totally unfounded. She could like Alan very much and enjoy being his friend, but that was as far as it would ever go for her, and for him, it might not be enough.

Alan was speaking again. 'You haven't explained yet what you were doing in the tower. I thought no one ever went in there.'

She looked at him in surprise. 'Not as far as I know—although Madame Bresson didn't seem awfully keen.'

'I'm not surprised. She probably thought she would come face to face with Marie-Denise.' He looked at Andrea's uncomprehending face. 'Don't tell me no one's told you about Marie-Denise?'

'I've never even heard the name mentioned,' she said, mildly exasperated. 'Is she someone I should know?'

All kinds of thoughts were racing through her mind. Was this Blaise's fiancée—the girl who had treated him so callously?

'Hardly—unless you were alive two hundred years ago. She was the wife of the Levallier of his day. There was a title then, but it disappeared at the time of the Revolution, and was never revived.' Alan looked rather pointedly at the floor. 'It was one of these arranged marriages. The couple never saw each other until the wedding day, apparently, and when they did see each other, they loathed each other on sight. Consequently when the Marquis returned to Versailles after his marriage, he left Marie-Denise here to enjoy her new status as Marquise on her own.'

'And did she—enjoy it?'

'She seems to have been a girl of spirit,' Alan conceded. 'She didn't take too long in finding consolation. In due course there was a baby—a little boy, which the Marquis could not possibly have fathered. Someone may have tipped him off, however, because he arrived home quite unexpectedly shortly afterwards. But Marie-Denise must have had a premonition, because the child was safely away from the chateau with his wet-nurse, and when the Marquis arrived everything seemed normal—the peasants quiet, and his wife dutiful. Whatever his information had been, it can't have been too specific, and he soon decided that someone had been playing a trick on him and went back to Paris.'

'How do you know all this?' Andrea asked, intrigued.

He shrugged. 'I told you I'd been studying local history. This is one of the unofficial stories everyone pushes in for free. I've heard at least half a dozen versions of it since I've been here, but they all stick to the same basic points. No one can actually prove who Marie-Denise's lover and the father of the child was, though. Some people say he was the son of a neighbouring landowner, but the most popular belief is that he was a man of the soil—one of the local peasantry—or even the Marquis's own major-domo.'

'Obviously a busy lady,' Andrea commented drily.

Alan smiled. 'Not in the way you think,' he said. 'Once she had the child, there was not another hint of scandal. And she was very popular—kind to her servants, good to the poor—in a way her husband was probably incapable of. Her secret became theirs. When the Marquis put in one of his infrequent appearances, the child was removed and looked after until he went away again.'

'But he must have found out?'

'Oh yes,' Alan said gravely. 'Marie-Denise must have had an enemy after all—perhaps the same person who told the Marquis originally. One day the Marquis took his departure—and came back later the same day. The child had returned by then, and he found them together in the tower. Marie-Denise was playing with the child and singing to him—and she looked up to see her husband standing in the doorway. She made some excuse—pretended it was a servant's child whom she was training to be her page, but he knew.'

'What did he say?'

'Nothing. He seems to have acted as if he believed her. That's what makes it so horrible really ...' He drank the remains of his tea and set the mug down. 'For about a week he played the devoted husband—toured the estate, gave dinner parties, talked to his tenants. Marie-Denise played her part too. It was too late to hide her son, but she made sure the little boy was kept out of his way. What the eye doesn't see, and all that ... But it was too late. One day when she went to the tower she found it locked, and the key gone. She wanted to know why, naturally. So her husband told her. The place was not safe, he said. Only that morning some servant's brat who must have gone in there to play had fallen out of one of the top windows and been killed in the courtyard.'

'Dear God!' Andrea stared at him, appalled. 'What did she do?'

'What could she do? She couldn't prove anything. It might even have been an accident. She had to go on with the pretence. She couldn't even mourn. This time when the Marquis went back to Paris, she went with him. They never returned to St Jean des Roches, but both died on the guillotine a few years later during the Terror. They had no children, and the chateau was inherited by a cousin. But the tradition that the tower should be kept locked persisted. Once it was unlocked, I was told, Marie-Denise would return to look for her son.'

Andrea shuddered. 'And Madame Bresson assured me there were no ghosts.'

'Nor are there,' Alan declared robustly. 'It's just a story. I haven't really scared you, have I?'

'No.' She summoned up a wan smile. 'But I was planning to use those rooms for a little boy—my—husband's nephew who is coming to live with us. I suppose I'll have to think again.'

'Oh, I don't know.' Alan busied himself with the teapot again. 'That's how these sort of superstitions gain credence. Using those rooms might be the best thing that could happen.'

'Hm.' Andrea was unconvinced. She now had an explanation for the housekeeper's agitation, and her insistence that Blaise should be consulted before any decision about the tower was made.

She got up, smoothing the creases out of her jeans. 'I'd better be going,' she said awkwardly. 'Thanks for the hospitality. You must have dinner with us at the chateau soon.'

Alan sent her a wry grin. 'Perhaps not too soon, but thanks for the thought. If I'm still around when the honeymoon is over, I hope you'll ask me again.'

She had an impulse to tell him that the honeymoon was over now—that it had never, in fact, begun, but something held her back. She had probably told Alan too much as it was. So she gave him a swift, meaningless smile and murmured goodbye.

Her thoughts were sombre as she walked back to the chateau. Marie-Denise's tragic story had affected her deeply, and she found herself wishing almost childishly that she had not had to hear it on her wedding day. It was not very encouraging to hear about another arranged marriage at the chateau which had gone so disastrously wrong.

Madame Bresson was hovering rather anxiously in the great hall when she appeared, and Andrea looked at her inquiringly.

Madame's own gaze was reproachful. 'Does Madame wish me to run her bath?' she asked.

Andrea realised that as far as the housekeeper was concerned, the honeymoon was in full swing, and that she was being given a none-too-subtle hint to dress for dinner. Her first impulse was to reply that she preferred to remain as she was, but she realised nothing would be gained by offending Madame Bresson's notion of correct behaviour, so she smiled and thanked her. In any case, the thought of a bath was not an unwelcome one. She was not so sure about dressing for dinner.

She had a dress, of course, popped into her case as an afterthought. Wool jersey in a glowing amber shade, cut on strictly mediaeval lines—long-sleeved and square-necked. And it did not come as a complete surprise, when she entered her room, to find it laid out across the bed. Her mind was being made up for her, it seemed.

When she was ready at last, she surveyed herself in the mirror. On the surface everything was fine. Her chestnut hair was looped smoothly back over her ears and tied at the nape of her neck by a length of chiffon the same shade as her dress. Gold fringed ear-rings swung from her ear-lobes. But it was her face that gave her away. The discreet make-up she had applied could not alleviate the underlying pallor induced by tension. Her eyes looked enormous and the soft curves of her mouth bore unmistakable signs of strain. She sighed. It was not the poised image she would have liked to present to the man who awaited her downstairs, but at least she would not have to contend with the revealing glare of electric light.

And tonight even the prosaic lamps had been dispensed with. The panelled walls gave back the more intimate glow of candlelight. Andrea checked in the doorway, fighting irritation and embarrassment. The room had been transformed into a setting for a lovers' tryst, and she would not have needed much prompting to turn around and flee back upstairs to the comparative security of her room. But common sense told her that it would be better to stay and try and behave as if she noticed nothing unusual. She must not let Blaise catch a glimpse of her inner disturbance, she thought almost frantically.

She walked across to the settle and sank down on to it,

holding out her hands to the leaping flames in the hearth. The crackling of the burning logs sounded like thunder in her ears, echoing the tumult of her own pulse beats.

More than anything she regretted this enforced intimacy. She wished now that she had persuaded Blaise to take her out—to the restaurant in Craudon that Alan had mentioned, perhaps—or that they had invited other guests to join them. But she was forced to admit that it was unlikely that anyone would have accepted such an invitation. It was assumed by everyone that they wanted to be alone. Any protestations to the contrary from her would be attributed to bridal nerves—which Blaise would soon have the means of curing. She had seen it in their eyes as they had come to congratulate them after the wedding ceremony, as she had stood beside Blaise, her hand resting formally on his arm—the age-old curiosity and speculation directed at every newly married pair.

Then, she had felt armoured in her own secret knowledge that they were all wrong, and that this marriage did not contain the elements their imagination were creating. Now, she was sure of nothing.

A sudden small sound disturbed her and she swung round, choking back the cry of alarm that her overcharged emotional state had brought to her lips. Blaise was standing at the end of the settle, one arm resting on its high carved back. His face was in shadow, so she could not read his expression, but she was immediately aware that he too had chosen to dress for the occasion, and to register how well the formality of his dark dinner jacket and white frilled shirt became him.

'You—you startled me.' Her voice sounded unaccustomedly breathless in her ears.

'*Evidémment,*' he said drily. 'I apologise. Perhaps I can make amends by getting you a drink.'

'Thank you,' she returned almost inaudibly. She took the glass he handed her, and sipped without the slightest awareness of the contents. Her hand was shaking so much she began to be afraid she would give herself away by spilling some of the liquid on her gown. But fortunately Blaise did not seem to notice her nervousness. She wondered how long he had been standing there before she had become aware of his presence. It disturbed her to think how vulnerable she had been under his scrutiny.

'Clothilde tells me you wish to use the tower rooms for Philippe.'

She looked up at him quickly, unable to gauge from his tone what his attitude might be.

'It seemed a good idea at the time,' she admitted. 'But now I'm not so sure.'

'Am I permitted to ask you why?'

She looked at him in surprise. 'I should have thought it was obvious. Once I'd heard about Marie-Denise . . .'

'Ah,' he said meditatively. 'So someone has told you that old story.'

'You don't believe it?'

He shrugged. 'Every old house has its stories of savagery and blood. Ours is no exception. But I would prefer they were not given undue importance. How much is truth and how much the product of fanciful minds is hard to tell at this distance.'

'Then can I go ahead?' she asked. 'It did seem ideal, but Madame Bresson thought . . .'

He smiled faintly. 'I will deal with Clothilde. As you can see,' he waved a hand rather derisively at the elaborately arranged dining table and the polished candelabra, 'she is the possessor of one of the fanciful minds I mentioned.'

Andrea felt the colour rise in her cheeks. 'I'd like to colour-wash the interior walls,' she said hurriedly. 'Cream, I think, or perhaps a pale yellow for warmth. And I'd like to buy a new bed for Philippe—a modern divan, I think, and some simple furniture.'

Blaise nodded. 'Order what you think will be best. I will tell Gaston to check the floors and ceilings—and the windows. Do you think bars should be fixed?'

'I don't like that idea. Philippe wouldn't be made to feel that he's a prisoner in any way. Perhaps Gaston could fit safety catches to the windows, so that they can be opened for ventilation just a little way.' She looked at him. 'Besides, bars at the windows would simply give credence to old superstitions.'

'Instead of which, we shall relegate them to the past where they belong.' He lifted his glass towards her in a mocking toast. '*Votre santé, madame.*'

She was saved having to reply by the entrance of Madame with the first course of their dinner. Tonight she had surpassed herself, Andrea thought as the clear soup was replaced by succulent prawns in a creamy sauce, to be followed in turn by chicken simmered with grapes in wine. In spite of her nervousness, the food was irresistible, and she ate with something very near her usual appetite. They drank champagne with the meal. The wine of celebration, she found herself thinking, and laid down her spoon, pushing her dessert plate away from her.

'Is something the matter?' Blaise's eyes seemed oddly watchful in the candelight.

'No,' she lied. 'I—I've just had enough to eat, that's all. Too much, really. I wasn't expecting such a banquet.'

'Ah.' Blaise leaned back in his chair, his dark face enigmatic. 'But Clothilde is of an old-fashioned tradition. She believes that good food and good wine means that—later—there will be good love.'

Andrea set her glass down again hurriedly. Her cheeks were crimson and she could think of nothing adequate to say in return.

'You are very quiet,' he observed after a pause, and she hated the sardonic amusement in his voice. 'It is possible that silence means consent, as your countrymen say?'

'No, it does not,' she made her voice as cold as possible. 'And I think under the circumstances, this conversation is in very poor taste.'

'What circumstances do you refer to, *ma mie*?' He poured some more wine into his glass.

'You know perfectly well.' She glared at him.

'I know that we were made man and wife today,' he said

reflectively. 'And that you look very beautiful, and that there is only the width of this table separating us.'

She pushed her chair back hastily, scraping the legs over the floor. 'There is far more than that between us, *monsieur*,' she said, unsuccessfully trying to control the tremor in her voice. 'It was a business arrangement that you offered and forced me to accept—nothing more.'

A faint smile brushed his lips. 'You deceive yourself, *ma chère*. The business arrangement, such as it was, I offered to your cousin Clare.'

Andrea stared at him, her heart hammering wildly. Then she got to her feet, her legs shaking under her. 'This has gone far enough,' she declared with more conviction than she was actually capable of feeling. 'That's pure sophistry and you know it. I agreed to a legal contract, that's all. There's not the slightest difference between that and the arrangement you made with Clare.'

'I hate to argue with you, *ma mie*,' he said coolly. 'But there is a marked difference. I have never, after all, held your cousin in my arms and felt her body tremble with desire.'

Andrea felt as if she were choking. 'How dare you!' she forced out at last. 'You have no right to say that ...'

'When you became my wife, you granted me any rights I chose to assert, Andrée.'

He stared up at her through half-closed eyes. The flickering candlelight playing on his scarred face gave him the look of a devil, she thought hysterically.

'I'll leave you, *monsieur*. Perhaps tomorrow you'll be in a more reasonable frame of mind.'

She made herself walk, not run, to the door. As she passed him, she had to resist an impulse to flinch away as if she was afraid he might lean out of his chair and seize her as she passed. But of course he did nothing of the sort. Only he laughed softly as she reached the door and went out.

She was halfway up the stairs when she realised he was coming after her. She stumbled over her long skirt as she tried to run, and snatched it up out of her way, damning it under her breath. Then he was beside her, and she was facing him, her back against the staircase wall. His hands rested on the wall on each side of her, not touching her. She could neither go up the stairs or down, and even without his imprisoning arms she knew that her trembling legs would not have obeyed her.

Pride would not serve her now. She whispered pleadingly, 'Blaise . . .' but her plea was stifled as his mouth came down on hers.

She would have welcomed brutality. It would have given her something to withstand, to fight against. His mouth was cool and gentle, almost teasing as he coaxed her lips apart, and then possessed of a devastating sensuality. Her head swam dizzily, and she lifted her hands, clinging to the lapels of his coat because otherwise she knew she would sink to the ground.

She never knew when kissing no longer became enough, but a convulsive sob of delight caught at her throat as the fierce demand of his hands sought and found her breasts. She had entertained an image of herself as cool and self-possessed. Now she was aware of needs within herself that terrified her. Yet it was not fear but a far older emotion that made her arch her slim body against his in an invitation more potent than any words.

He lifted her into his arms as easily as if she had been a featherweight. She turned her face against his chest, not caring where he was taking her, savouring the warmth of his skin through his shirt.

A small measure of sanity returned when she was set gently to her feet and knew that they were in his room. Now, if ever, she had to rally her defences against him—to protest. But even as she registered the thought, she felt her dress slip from her body to the floor, and knew that all protest was much, much too late.

Lying on the bed beside him, she gave herself up to his kisses. His hands were exploring her body with a heart-stopping intimacy which seemed to make even the most fragile of underclothing an indefensible intrusion—a barrier which could and should be swept away.

Yet when it was done, a sudden paralysing shyness overwhelmed her. She wasn't ashamed of her body—of course she wasn't. She wanted him to look at her. But he was the first man who had ever seen her—like this, and she couldn't meet his gaze. She turned her face away and closed her eyes, longing for him to kiss and caress her again, and dissolve away her shyness for ever.

But he neither kissed nor touched her, and with a swift quiver of awareness she realised that he was no longer beside her. Her eyes flew open.

He was standing by the bed, looking down at her, his face filled with a cold anger that terrified her. The fact that he was still fully dressed made it all, somehow, so much worse . . .

'Cover yourself with this, *madame*.' As if he could read her thoughts, he tossed something down to her. It drifted across her body, a ripple of white lace torn to shreds. She gave a little horrified gasp, then was mute as he spoke again, his words falling like so many lashes with a whip across her quivering senses.

'I promised I would teach you a lesson, *ma mie*. Maybe we have both learned something. At least you will treat any future gifts from me with a little more respect. I wish you goodnight.'

He turned and strode away from her across the room, and Andrea heard the door shut behind him.

CHAPTER SIX

It was very early the next morning when Andrea awoke. For a moment or two she lay, her fingers pressed against her throbbing head, wondering why she had woken, and why she felt so wretched, and then memory came flooding back, and she knew.

She could not cry any more. She had shed enough tears the previous night, after she had stumbled back from Blaise's room. She still found it difficult to believe that he could have treated her with such diabolical cruelty. He had made her want him, forced a total, aching response from her, and then rejected her. Surely her destruction of the nightgown he had given her had not warranted such an utter humiliation in return?

And it was little satisfaction to know that his plan had misfired, and that his body had tricked him into desiring her too. At the very moment when she had been ready to give herself to him, he had been cold-blooded enough to draw back, in spite of everything that had passed between them.

It was useless too to tell herself that if he had in fact made love to her, merely to appease a cynical desire for a woman, she would have even more to regret at this moment. How would she have felt, waking to the knowledge that she had been used because the woman he really loved and wanted was lost to him?

The thought was like a physical blow. What a fool she'd been! There had been moments in Blaise's arms when she would have sworn there was real tenderness commingled with his passion. Yet not even the passion had been real. He had merely been 'teaching her a lesson.'

More sleep was impossible, she thought, swinging her legs out of bed and searching for her embroidered mules. When she was calmer—when the hurt was less, then she would decide what to do. She had promised Blaise a year of her life, but that was no longer feasible. She could not stay at the chateau after this. She supposed she would have to remain until Philippe arrived, so that the legality of his guardianship could be established without question, but once the boy had settled in she would go. Blaise could say she had gone to England to visit her relations, make up any story he pleased, she thought bitterly. He had shown a total lack of regard for her feelings. Why should she now consider his?

She washed and dressed herself quickly in jeans and a

sweater. Her soft leather shoes made hardly a sound on the stairs as she descended and made her way to the kitchen. There was no sign of Madame Bresson. It was too early even for her to be around, although Andrea heard a faint noise somewhere in the distance which might have been Gaston chopping sticks. She set the stove glowing and found the coffee pot and a jar of coffee. When it was ready, she sweetened the brew and drank it black, sitting at the big scrubbed table.

It occurred to her that she had not yet written to Clare to tell her what had happened. As things were, she might well arrive back in London ahead of any letter, she thought with a brief, unhappy sign. It would have been easy to blame Clare for her present desolation, but in her heart she knew that it would be unjust. She had had few illusions when she set out on this escapade about the risks she would be running. And while she had been able to convince herself that she had agreed to marry Blaise solely for Uncle Max's sake, she now knew only too well that it had been a piece of useless self-deception. She had been fighting her attraction to Blaise almost from the moment she had entered his house. Clare's piece of foolishness had been an excuse to stay, however good her intentions might have been initially. Once she had seen the calibre of the man she had crossed swords with, she should have run. But she had stayed, telling herself it was for Clare—for Uncle Max, when the truth was it all for herself. This truth had been forced on her last night, when she had lain in Blaise's arms and known in his lovemaking the culmination of every dream of delight she had ever experienced. Yet all the time she had been caught in a trap of her own devising.

She grimaced slightly as she drained her cup down to the dregs. She rinsed it out in the sink and left it to dry on the wide draining board. She would go back to her room, she decided, and write to Clare and her aunt, giving them a severely edited version of what had transpired. It was pointless telling them not to worry, she knew philosophically, but at least she could give them the reassurance that she would be home very soon, for good.

She was walking back through the great hall when she heard someone moving about. For a moment she thought it was Madame Bresson and nerved herself to meet an interrogation as to why she was up so early on the day after her wedding.

The dining room door opened suddenly with a jerk, and Blaise stood framed in the doorway. His dinner jacket was slung carelessly over one shoulder, his tie was gone, and his once elegant shirt hung open to the waist. His hair was dishevelled and a dark stubble of beard showed on his chin. His eyes were bloodshot, and as they met Andrea's they narrowed slightly, as if he was having difficulty in focusing.

Looking past him, Andrea could see an empty whisky bottle and a glass on the table.

'Good morning, *madame*.' His articulation was a little too careful. 'I trust you slept well?'

For a long traitorous moment she let her memory run back, feeling again his body, hard with desire, against her own, re-living the touch of his mouth, tasting the scent of his skin. Then she crushed the feelings down and let pride and hurt and anger have their way.

'At least I didn't need the help of alcohol,' she retorted, lifting her chin defiantly.

He grinned sardonically and waved a hand in the direction of the bottle. 'You are familiar with the tradition of the bachelor night, are you not? I preferred to have mine after the ceremony rather than before it, that is all.'

She shrugged scornfully. 'You don't have to explain yourself to me, *monsieur*. If you wish to degrade yourself by getting drunk, it's your own affair.'

'Don't provoke me, *ma mie*,' he said between his teeth. 'Didn't last night's lesson teach you it could be dangerous?'

She gave a slight shrug, turning away deliberately towards the stairs in an attempt to conceal the emotion she was afraid he might read too frankly in her eyes.

'I didn't mean to be provocative,' she said wearily, at last. 'It really isn't any concern of mine what you do. At least we can guarantee not to interfere in each other's lives while I am here.'

'I think you deceive yourself, Andrée. I promise I shall not hesitate to interfere if your conduct does not meet with my satisfaction.' He walked over to her and stood studying her averted face rather grimly. 'Following from this, I would prefer you to—curtail, shall we say?—your visits to the gatehouse.'

Startled, she looked up at him, her eyes blazing. 'I'll do nothing of the sort! You have no right to expect . . .'

'I have every right,' he interrupted, his tone hardening perceptibly. 'You are my wife, and you will behave in an appropriate manner.'

'There is nothing—inappropriate about my meeting Alan Woodhouse,' she flashed. 'I find him pleasant company, that's all.'

'It could well be enough.'

'Oh, I don't believe this is happening,' she shook her head impatiently. 'We're fellow countrymen, alone in a strange place. It's natural we should seek each other out occasionally—surely you can see that?'

'I can see that and beyond,' he said curtly. His fingers gripped her chin bruisingly, making her meet his gaze. 'I warn you, Andrée, obey me in this or your young compatriot will have to find another refuge in which to pursue his researches.'

'That's the most unfair thing I've ever heard!' she wrenched herself free of his clasp. 'My God, anyone who heard you would actually think you were jealous, instead of . . .' she paused.

'Instead of what?' he prompted her too pleasantly.

'A dog in the manger, I suppose,' she said rather lamely.

'Warning everyone else away from what I do not myself desire?' He smiled mirthlessly. 'Perhaps, but don't be mistaken, *ma mie*. My bite is infinitely worse than my bark, as you have come near to discovering on more than one occasion. Accept this as a friendly warning, and act upon it.'

'What have either of us to do with friendship?' she asked

almost despairingly, and could have bitten back the words as soon as they were uttered. Something flickered for an instant in his eyes, but his voice was quite calm when he spoke.

'Probably very little, you are right. Maybe mutual toleration is the best we can hope for.' He pushed a hand through his dark hair, stretching wearily. Andrea turned away and began to mount the stairs.

'I made some coffee,' she tossed back over her shoulder at him. 'It will probably still be hot.'

'You overwhelm me, *ma mie*,' he returned mockingly. 'What a dutiful wife you might have made under happier circumstances!'

He waited for a moment as if expecting some retort, then laughed softly as he walked away.

Andrea came down the steps from the upper room of the tower and stood looking around her with a certain amount of quiet satisfaction. Two weeks of concentrated hard work had certainly paid off. With Gaston's admittedly reluctant assistance, she had cleared the lumber out of the ground floor room, and covered the discolouring plaster in a warm oatmeal shade. There was rush matting on the floor, and gay cotton curtains in a mixture of red, violet and white at the windows. She had covered flat cushions to match and put them into the deep window embrasures to act as informal seating. Gaston had unearthed a large rather ugly cupboard from some recess, and this, now painted white, waited to house Philippe's toys and books. Andrea had been unsure whether she was expected to supply these as well, but she was unwilling to approach Blaise and ask him. He had not expressed the slightest interest in her activities in the tower so far, which increased her reluctance to involve him. She had no wish for him to think that she was seeking his attention or his praise.

She had kept her spending rigidly to a minimum. The main expenditure had been on the little divan bed, which had had to be transported in sections up to the upper room by the sweating Gaston. The simple chest of drawers and clothes cupboard had been kits which she had managed to assemble herself after a short struggle.

Gaston had obtained the window catches she wanted and fixed them, and he had also securely screwed down the trapdoor which led from Philippe's bedroom to the floor. He did not say so, and Andrea did not ask, but she guessed this was where the legend stated that Marie-Denise's child had fallen or been pushed to his death. There was an oddly desolate air in the room that even the pigeons lodging in the rafters could not disseminate, and she was glad it was so firmly blocked off.

It had been a strange task, preparing these rooms for a child she had never seen. She had wondered about him a great deal as she worked, glad of the preoccupation to keep her mind from more personal matters. Blaise had been non-committal about him, saying merely he had been little more than a baby when he last saw him, and inclined to cry a great deal.

Andrea felt he was not really very interested in the boy, and she wondered why he was so determined to secure his guardianship if this was the case. Was it merely the same possessive instinct she had seen demonstrated towards herself? If so, it was a disturbing atmosphere for such a young child to have to cope with.

If it was just a sense of duty towards his dead brother which was prompting him, she felt even more uneasy. Duty was such a cold-sounding word in this context. She wondered if Philippe might not really be better off with the aunt who was looking after him. Presumably she was capable of some warmer feeling towards him—the affection that a child robbed of both his parents so obviously needed.

She doubted, with a pang, whether Blaise was able to give Philippe the loving environment he deserved. He could feel passion, she knew, but she had seen little sign of any gentler side to his emotional make-up. Did it even exist behind that wall of cool, mocking politeness that he generally showed her? She often thought she had imagined those brief moments in his arms when he had shown her what tenderness could be. Now he was at a distance again, the aloof, mocking stranger making it clear that his personality was as scarred as his face.

She gave a little sigh, absent-mindedly smoothing a fold in one of the curtains. A disturbing picture had forced itself upon her inner consciousness—Blaise, his face miraculously softened and gentle, looking down at the child he held in his arms—not an orphan needing his shelter and support, but his own child. She crossed her arms on her breasts, feeling once again the pain of rejection. Why did she torment herself like this? Blaise did not want her—he had made that more than clear. He had proved beyond all doubting her total vulnerability, and his indifference. He did not need her in his bed, or in his life, and as soon as she had ceased to be useful to him, he would let her go without regret. Somehow she hoped by reiterating the position to herself, she might make it hurt less, but she had to admit that so far she had been wholly unsuccessful.

Blaise had taught her a woman's desires, but denied her their fulfilment, and in some strange way she knew that no matter how many miles or years might part them in the future, she would never be free of him because of this.

She gave a little shiver and left the tower, closing the door behind her. She wandered restlessly into the main building, and stood in the great hall, looking round her with critical eyes. Now that Philippe's rooms were completed, she would have more time to spend on the rooms they used in the chateau. Refurbishing the great hall would be a major undertaking, but it occurred to her there was one thing she could do to give it a more welcoming appearance. Determinedly she went off to the kitchen quarters to seek out Gaston. She found him sitting at the table, drinking a large bowl of coffee, surrounded by all the preparations for the evening meal which Madame Bresson had left ready before going down to the village to give one of her lace-making lessons.

Andrea had to admit she found Gaston heavy going at

times. His command of English was non-existent, and she had to persevere very hard in French to get him to understand anything she said. Sometimes she suspected he was being deliberately obtuse, taking a childish delight in seeing her searching for the right word or phrase to make her meaning clearer to him.

Today his eyes surveyed her guilessly over the top of the bowl and he grinned happily.

'It will snow soon, I think, *madame*,' he announced almost gleefully.

'Oh, no!' Andrea peered out of the window in dismay. The sky was massed with clouds, it was true, but she could not see the leaden look which usually presaged a snowfall. Yet at the same time, she had been aware all day that the temperature had dropped considerably.

Gaston nodded. '*Une forte chute de neige*,' he prophesied. '*La route au village sera bloquée*.'

That was all she needed, Andrea thought resignedly, to be snowed up. She enjoyed her walks to the village and round the surrounding countryside, and she had imagined taking Philippe with her. Apart from anything else, it was the excuse she needed to get away from the chateau and the disturbing presence of its master. Now it seemed likely she would be thrust into his company, maybe for days on end. She had heard that many of the small side roads in Auvergne were sometimes completely closed off in bad weather, but she had not imagined it happening quite so early in the year. Besides, if the roads were blocked by snow, this could also mean Philippe would be delayed in arriving at St Jean des Roches. As it was, she knew Blaise had not been officially informed of his probable date of arrival, but she had assumed it could not be long in coming and had been working more or less against the clock to ensure that everything was ready and welcoming for him when he did come.

She turned to Gaston. 'I'd like you to light a fire in the hall,' she said.

He stared at her, twisting his face up as if he had suddenly been afflicted by deafness, and patiently she repeated her request. To her amazement she saw that he was shaking his head.

'*Non, madame. Ce n'est pas possible.* No fire there, never.'

'It's perfectly possible,' Andrea retorted. 'I've never seen a bigger fireplace. A fire would make the whole place less gloomy. *Pas si sombre*,' she added for emphasis, as Gaston was still shaking his head in a woebegone manner.

With a mixture of irritation and amusement, Andrea guessed he was envisaging the stack of extra kindling wood and logs that would be required. The additional work wouldn't really do him any harm, she thought, viewing his tubby frame disparagingly.

'You can start chopping the sticks as soon as you've finished your coffee,' she decreed.

While she was waiting, she washed down the carved stone work, and scrubbed the hearth itself. The glow of a fire was just what this great barn of a place needed, she told herself optimistically, as Gaston trudged in with a basket of kindling wood on his arm and an air of almost tangible disapproval.

'*Il faut ramoner, madame*,' he informed her, scowling.

Whatever that means, Andrea thought tartly. She gave him a sweet smile.

'I know what I'm doing, Gaston. And it will make the whole house warmer, I promise you.'

Gaston shrugged, apparently fatalistically, and set the basket of sticks down beside her. Andrea laid the fire neatly and set a match to it. The sticks were dry and flared up at once, and she laid larger pieces of wood on top of them, placing a small log on top of the pile for good measure.

'There,' she stood up smiling, brushing off her trousers with her hands. 'That looks more cheerful already.'

The words were hardly uttered when a great gust of smoke blew back into the hall, enveloping her. Choking, and her eyes streaming, Andrea backed away, but not far enough to escape the fall of soot which slid out of the big chimney with a subdued roar, extinguishing the fire in a reeking cloud which spread, covering all the neighbouring surfaces, including Andrea herself.

'Oh, *hell*!' Almost crying with vexation, she retreated back out of range of any further falls and looked down at her soot-encrusted clothes with horror. She could imagine what her face and hair looked like. She swung on Gaston, and disturbed something suspiciously like a smirk on his face.

'Well, don't just stand there!' she began almost hysterically, then checked, transfixed by a new and unexpected sound—a car horn in the courtyard outside. Visitors, she thought with something like despair. And what was Blaise going to say when he came to greet them and found his hall like a charcoal-burner's hut, and his wife looking like a refugee from the Black and White Minstrels?

Gaston looked at her, shaking his head again sadly. '*Il faut ramoner la cheminée, madame*,' he muttered regretfully.

'I get it,' Andrea said grimly. 'The chimney needs sweeping! And so do I.'

She turned and headed frantically for the stairs, in an attempt to make her escape before the unknown callers gained admittance. But she was too late. As she reached the foot of the staircase the great door swung open to reveal Blaise himself ushering in a young woman and a small boy. In spite of herself, Andrea paused, realising that this must be Philippe come at last and unannounced.

The child saw her too, and his finger pointed.

'*Qu'est-ce que c'est que ça?*' he demanded unanswerably in a shrill treble.

Groaning inwardly, Andrea saw a look of furious anger replace the astonishment on Blaise's face. At the same time she registered almost dazedly the exotic beauty of his companion. She was not tall, but perfectly made and exquisitely dressed. Her hair was raven black, cut in a sleek pageboy which curved with the line of her jaw and slanting dark eyes were set in a face which would have rivalled a magnolia. Those eyes now were filled with amazement and a sly contempt which set Andrea's overtried nerves jangling. The full lips pouted derisively as she turned to Blaise.

'Aren't you going to present me to your wife, *mon chéri*?' Her voice, husky and intimately pitched, matched her appearance, but Andrea unerringly detected the note of malice it contained.

'*Certainement*.' Blaise strode forward, his face like a stone mask. He took Andrea's arm, his fingers biting into her flesh. 'Andrée, permit me to introduce Simone Delatour, Philippe's aunt.'

Andrea forced a smile, furiously aware of the disadvantage she was placed in. She could not even offer her hand to Simone.

'I'm sorry you should have had such a welcome, *mademoiselle*.' She spoke with more warmth than she actually felt. 'You—you've taken us rather by surprise, I'm afraid.'

'Blaise must have forgotten to mention it.' The other girl's smile widened, but Andrea felt instinctively it was directed at her rather than with her. She turned to him. 'You did get my letter—didn't you, *chéri*?'

Andrea tensed. Blaise had received a letter from Simone telling him that she was bringing Philippe in person and had failed to mention it to her? She stifled a furious gasp. Surely he realised the extra preparations such a visit would entail, and he knew how busy she had been getting Philippe's rooms ready. Now, it appeared, she would have to start again. She could have burst into tears.

His hand was still heavy on her arm, but she released herself with an effort.

'Perhaps you'll excuse me now,' she said, thankful there was no betraying quiver in her voice. 'I—I have rather a lot to do.'

'I think you're forgetting something.' Blaise's voice was like a whiplash. 'You have not yet greeted your new nephew.'

Andrea groaned inwardly in dismay. She turned to the little boy who had stood silently all this time, and looked at him. He was not the most attractive child she had ever seen, thin and rather sallow, his dark hair standing out in wisps from his head. The round dark eyes, she saw unhappily, were regarding her with unmistakable hostility.

'Philippe.' She held out her arms encouragingly. 'If you wouldn't mind a rather sooty hug . . .'

She got no further. With a loud wail Philippe Levallier ran to Simone and buried his head in her skirt. '*Ma tante!*' he sobbed.

Andrea bit her lip. She had never fooled herself into thinking that there could be instant affection between Philippe and herself, but she had not bargained for this outright rejection either. She did not dare look at Blaise to see what effect Philippe's action had had on him. She murmured something hasty about washing and ran for the stairs.

She went into the bathroom, trying to touch as little as possible, and turned on the bath-taps, shedding her clothes with an almost desperate urgency.

When she was clean again, she began to feel calmer. Her hair had also shared the general rinsing process, and she took the towel that hung over the side of the bath and began to rub it dry. Dinner was no problem, she thought. There was always plenty of food, and Madame Bresson would have returned by now. She could leave all that side of things safely to her. But she felt utterly defeated at the thought of turning out one of those large gloomy bedrooms to accommodate Simone, whose entire appearance and attitude suggested that she expected and was accustomed to receive nothing but the best.

She sighed. Skulking here in the bathroom in rapidly cooling water was going to solve nothing, she told herself, reaching for her large towel in preparation for getting out. Her hand froze into stillness as the bathroom door swung open and Blaise strode in.

For a second she regarded him in sheer open-mouthed outrage, then, galvanised into frantic activity, she dragged the towel across herself, regardless of the fact that most of it joined her in the grimy water.

'How dare you!' she choked.

His brows snapped together menacingly. 'Don't be a child,' he said coldly. 'The sight of a naked woman is not a total novelty to me, and a few centimetres of soot-encrusted bathwater scarcely constitutes an allurement, I promise you. I have come to tell you that Madame Bresson is at this moment transferring your clothes from your room in order to prepare it for Simone.'

'Oh.' Andrea digested this for a moment. It was a solution she supposed—as long as it did not rain too hard. 'And which room am I to occupy?'

He paused. Then 'Mine,' he said curtly.

She stared at him, the towel almost slipping momentarily from her suddenly nerveless fingers.

'You're joking,' she said at last very quietly.

'I was never more serious in my life.' He flung up a hand sardonically. 'Oh, spare me the hysteria. It's not an arrangement I would have chosen, believe me, but I have reasons for wishing Simone to suppose our marriage is—a normal one in every way. She would be unlikely to think that if she discovered we occupied separate bedrooms almost at opposite ends of the house.'

'But there must be some other answer,' she said unevenly, feeling her pulses throbbing uncertainly. 'An adjoining room—something, surely.'

His lips twisted sneeringly. 'A convenient dressing room, no doubt. I'm afraid I don't possess such a refinement. But you need have no fears. You may have overlooked the fact that the room does have a couch. I shall sleep on that.'

She swallowed. 'This is ludicrous! Our marriage has fulfilled the legal qualification you needed. The precise nature of our relationship has nothing to do with anyone else.'

She nearly added, 'Least of all Simone,' but something—she didn't know what—stopped her.

'I have told you, I have my reasons.' In spite of the intimacy of their confrontation, his face and voice were as remote as if they had been a thousand miles apart.

'And I think I have a right to know what they are.' The

water was almost cold now, and she had to repress a shiver.

'Don't let us talk of rights, *ma mie*.' His tone took on a dangerous softness. 'But if you insist, I'll admit that one of my reasons is pride.' He looked down into her widening eyes and gave a short, savage laugh. 'Amusing, is it not, that I am not sufficiently inured to my—affliction to be able to accept calmly that you find the sight of me repulsive. I had thought I was cured of all such foolishness, but you taught me differently, did you not, *mon ange*? However, I would prefer that it remained our secret, so you will share my room while Simone remains with us, and thank whatever God you believe in that I will demand no more of you.'

'You knew this was going to happen, didn't you?' she challenged him, her teeth beginning to chatter in spite of herself. 'You knew that Simone was coming with Philippe and that this situation would arise, and you deliberately didn't tell me, so that you could present me with this—*fait accompli*.'

'Don't torture your little mind.' Anger flamed in his eyes. 'This is no Machiavellian plot to get you into my bed. Yes, Simone did say that she would accompany Philippe here, but I thought it was an idle threat. However, she prides herself on her—unpredictability, shall we say?' He looked at her, his eyes narrowing. 'You're shivering. Name of God, you little fool!'

He stepped forward and before she could say or do anything to prevent him, scooped her out of the bath, regardless of damp hair or the dripping towel.

For a brief moment she was held against him, every clamouring nerve in her body registering the warmth of his skin through his shirt. It took all the self-control of which she was capable to stop her pressing herself against him, sliding her hands inside the open neck of his shirt to draw that warmth even closer.

Then he set her roughly on her feet. 'Dry yourself, *madame*,' he advised curtly. 'You have guests waiting for you downstairs, and Philippe has not yet seen his rooms.'

In spite of the turmoil ensuing from the changeover of rooms, Andrea managed to rescue a pair of corded velvet trousers in dark green and a white polo-necked sweater. She could not compete with Simone's sophisticated chic, so it was foolish to try, she told herself. But she felt taut and nervous as she descended the stairs. Most of the soot had gone by now, she noticed. Presumably Gaston had cleared it away, she decided rather morosely.

She pushed open the dining room door and went in. It was a cosy enough scene. Simone was seated by the fire, cigarette in hand, with a cup of coffee, while Philippe was up at the table, both hands clasped firmly round a mug of milk. Andrea smiled, trying to smother an instinctive feeling of nervousness. She seemed to have got off on the wrong foot with Philippe, but there was plenty of time for matters to improve, and after all, he was little more than a baby.

She glanced at Simone and saw with a flicker of resentment the look of disparagement to which the other girl was subjecting her surroundings. Almost in spite of herself, she felt an upsurge of pride of ownership. The furniture might be old and shabby, and the hangings drab and threadbare, but was Simone blind to the mellowness of the panelled walls, and the romance of the small leaded panes in the windows? The worn flags of the floor and the ancient stonework of the hearth had a charm all their own too. Andrea lifted her chin a little.

'Is this your first visit to St Jean des Roches, *mademoiselle*?' she asked politely.

There was a trace of amusement in the slanting cats-eyes that turned unblinkingly towards her.

'I am happy to say it is.' Simone made a slight, delicate gesture with her cigarette. 'It is not exactly the *milieu* I would choose. But we must not be so formal, you and I. You must call me Simone, and I will call you—what is it Blaise says?—Andrée.'

Andrea murmured courteously in the affirmative in response, but instinctively she knew she had little desire for an informal relationship with Simone. She felt in her bones that they could never be friends.

'I thought Philippe might care to see his rooms now.' She turned towards him with an encouraging smile.

Philippe stared back at her, his expression mutinous. 'I have not yet finished my milk,' he stated clearly.

'So I see,' Andrea returned equably. 'There is no hurry. Take as long as you like.'

He set the mug down pettishly, spilling a few drops on to the polished surface of the table.

'I do not wish to drink any more.' He slid off his chair, his eyes fixed on Simone. 'Will you come too, *ma tante*?'

Simone shrugged gracefully. 'If you wish, *mon petit*.' She rose to her feet in one sleek fluid motion, tossing the remains of her cigarette into the fire. She smiled faintly at Andrea. 'You do not object, I hope? I do not intrude.'

'Of course not,' Andrea assured her rather woodenly. It was stupid to feel put out over such a little thing. Nothing was going as she planned. She had imagined as she prepared the rooms showing them to Philippe, watching his face—but not, somehow, in front of an audience—and certainly not an inimical one as Simone undoubtedly was in spite of her appearance of friendliness. She must not forget that Simone had fought to retain control of Philippe, and it was thanks to herself that she had lost that fight. There was no reason for Simone to cherish any sort of amiable feelings towards her, unless, of course, she was determined to put a good face on her defeat. But somehow she did not strike Andrea as being a good loser . . .

Gaston had carefully oiled the hinges so the tower door no longer squealed like a lost soul when it was pushed open.

Andrea extended a coaxing hand to Philippe. 'Welcome to your domain, *monsieur*.'

Philippe ignored the overture. He thrust his own hands into the pockets of his shorts and stepped alone over the threshold. Andrea followed, feeling snubbed. She did not have to look at Simone to know that somewhere, not far from the surface, a gleam of triumph lurked.

Philippe surveyed his new surroundings, his head thrown back. His face was curiously devoid of emotion, a little blank mask totally at variance with his child's body. He turned to Andrea.

'There is more, *madame*?' he inquired.

Rather helplessly, Andrea led the way across to the stairs, and they ascended them in silence, Simone bringing up the rear.

Again the child stood quite quietly, looking around him. His round dark eyes took in the new bed, with its vividly patterned quilt and the toning linen pillowcase, and the gleaming modern furnishings. He walked across to the windows and knelt up on the embrasure, looking out. He touched the curtains and registered that they were the same pattern as the quilt. Something stirred in his face, shattering that too-adult air of restraint he wore.

He took a breath. 'You—did all this—for me, *madame*?'

There was a sudden, inexplicable lump in Andrea's throat.

She replied gravely, 'All for you, Philippe.'

He looked at her as if he was seeing her for the first time. Somewhere Andrea thought she glimpsed just the beginnings of a fugitive smile, then Simone said from the doorway, almost idly;

'It's a long way from the rest of the house, *mon chou*. Are you sure you won't be frightened to be all alone?'

In a flash, the old shuttered look came back into the little face. Philippe lifted his shoulders awkwardly, then ran past Andrea to Simone, burying his face in her dress as he had done earlier.

Over his head, Simone regarded her calmly. 'He is a very nervous child,' she said.

When he's reminded to be. The thought came to Andrea unbidden as she looked at the back of the small dark head. She knew with utter conviction that Philippe had been childishly relishing the sheer unconventionality of his strange, circular bedroom, until Simone had spoken. And she knew with a sinking heart as she looked at the other girl's quietly smiling face that though Simone might concede a battle lost, the war over Philippe was far from concluded.

Andrea felt distinctly odd as she changed for dinner that evening. It was a strange and in some ways disturbing thing to see her clothes hanging next to Blaise's in the big old-fashioned wardrobe, and to know that he had the right to enter the room at any time. It was a realisation that made her fingers suddenly clumsy as she coped with zips and hooks, and she told herself she was being a fool as she hurried into her long amber gown. Blaise had seen her, after all, much less than even half dressed.

It was disturbing too to see that there were now two pillows on the big bed. In spite of Blaise's reassurances that he intended to sleep on the hard-looking *chaise-longue* which stood in the window recess, Andrea felt flutterings of apprehension in the pit of her stomach. Life, she had discovered, was much less painful while she managed to keep out of his way. Now, it seemed, she was to be thrust into intimate proximity with him, and the realisation that his reluctance probably exceeded her own did not help the situation in any way, she thought.

She looked in the mirror at herself and grimaced slightly. What was she doing dressed up like this? Trying to compete, for heaven's sake? With whom and for what? She tried to laugh at her own absurdity, but the laugh sounded more like a sob in her own ears.

Simone was already in occupation in the dining room when Andrea went down. The heavy scent she wore seemed to dominate the small room, and the dress she wore, demurely high at the front and plunging wellnigh to disaster at the back, was just too sophisticated for her surroundings. All the stops had been pulled out, and no mistake! Beside her on the settle, Philippe looked small and somehow extinguished, but he looked up at her as she talked and gestured and laughed like a devotee at a shrine.

Blaise turned slightly as Andrea came in, and their eyes met and held for what seemed an endless moment. Then he smiled faintly and lifted the glass he held in a half-toast. Obeying an instinct she barely understood, Andrea walked across the room to his side and lifted her face to his with an assurance she was far from feeling. There was an almost imperceptible hesitation, then he bent and brushed his mouth briefly across hers in the most conventional of salutes. As she stepped back from him, Andrea caught Simone's eyes watching them, narrowed like a snake's, she thought, appalled. Then Simone was smiling and reaching for another cigarette and asking for a light, charmingly plaintive, and Andrea thought she must have been imagining things.

Then the other girl made a *moue* and picked up her bag again.

'I found this on the floor in my room, Andrée. I assume it's yours. I cannot imagine that Clothilde has taken to cosmetics at this stage in her life.'

It was a lipstick in a plain gold case, Clare's last birthday present to her, Andrea realised. She was wearing lip gloss instead that evening, or she would have missed it herself. She made herself smile.

'Thank you. I—I used that room myself before Blaise and I were married. I must have lost it then.'

Simone's arched brows rose in exaggerated surprise. 'But such a charming shade. How could you bear to be without it? I would have torn the chateau down stone by stone to find it again.'

Andrea could feel her cheeks burning. She gave a little shrug.

'I have to confess I don't bother a great deal with make-up since I've been here.'

'No, you prefer soot, do you not?' Only another woman would have scented the underlying malice in the joking remark. 'A bizarre beauty treatment, *ma chère*, but it seems to work. You have the English complexion that is the envy of the world.' She sent a slanting glance at Blaise. 'Your tastes have changed, *mon chéri*. At one time you did not admire that clean, scrubbed look.'

Making her sound, Andrea thought, seething, about as alluring as a cake of carbolic soap.

She was thankful for Madame Bresson who arrived at that moment to serve the soup.

Conversation over dinner turned, to Andrea's relief, from the personal to the general. One of the main topics was the farming co-operative, on which Simone seemed surprisingly well informed. It was unexpected to say the least to hear those exquisitely curved and painted lips uttering intelligent comments on crop yields and breeding strains.

Andrea felt almost ashamed that she herself knew so little about the co-operative. It wasn't that she was uninterested, she told herself defensively. She had been so busy in the house that there was very little time for anything else. Besides, the person to tell her all she needed to know about the estate was obviously Blaise—and him she had to avoid.

She set herself to draw Philippe out, but the little boy was obviously tired and disinclined to answer questions, and her efforts were abortive. The delicious meal seemed curiously tasteless suddenly and she picked up her wine glass and drank, trying to banish the feeling of *malaise* which was plaguing her.

She had been so intent on Philippe that she had not been listening to Simone's conversation with Blaise, but her attention was seized suddenly by an exchange that set off questions in her own mind.

'But how can you say that?' Simone was expostulating. 'Why, at Belle Rivière it was . . .'

'Belle Rivière has gone for ever,' Blaise interrupted, his voice harsh and strained as if her words had revived unbearable memories. 'We will not draw comparisons from that, if you please.'

Simone gave him an oblique glance and laid down her fork.

'As you please.' Her tone was meek, but Andrea was left

with the strongest impression that she was not entirely displeased with the reaction her words had provoked.

At her side, Philippe gave vent to a cavernous yawn which he imperfectly tried to conceal behind his hand.

Andrea pushed back her chair. 'This poor child is almost asleep on his feet,' she mentioned. 'If you'll excuse me, I'll put him to bed.'

'Oh, let me.' Simone rose, crumpling her table napkin. Her eyes by some alchemy looked enormous and her mouth drooped wistfully. 'It may be the last time I shall be able to tuck him into bed and tell him a story. You will have the rest of his childhood to enjoy. Don't deny me this, Andrée, *je vous en prie*.'

Andrea immediately felt at a disadvantage, as if she was deliberately grudging Philippe's aunt a few last moments of his company. And it was true, she was being deprived of the child. Weakly, she heard herself assenting and saw Philippe led off by Simone, who gave them both one of her slant-eyed smiles from the doorway.

She sank back into her chair, feeling a little crushed, and was startled to hear a muffled imprecation from Blaise.

'Why did you let her do that?' he demanded violently. 'It was your place to put Philippe to bed.'

Andrea had an overwhelming urge to put her head down on the table and weep.

'What harm can it do?' she defended herself. 'You have the custody of him now, so you can afford to be generous. Anyway, children enjoy these night-time rituals, and if it helps Philippe settle in more happily ...' She shrugged and left the sentence incomplete. Uncomfortably, she was remembering Simone's comments on the comparative isolation of the tower room and how Philippe had reacted to this, but Blaise was angry enough as it was, and she did not want to add further fuel to the flames by telling him this.

He did not reply, but, stealing a glance at him, she saw his face was set in lines of anger, and she gave a quick, inward sigh. Her heart ached for little Philippe. He obviously worshipped Simone, and now he was going to be parted from her—a shattering blow to his security that might have been redeemed by a stable environment in his new home, with his new aunt and uncle. Yet what was going to happen? In a year, maybe less, she would be gone and his life would be disrupted again. And what kind of life would he have once he and Blaise were alone? Would he end up as bleak and cynical as his uncle, seemingly incapable of normal emotions?

She drank what little wine remained in her glass and determinedly rose.

'If you'll excuse me,' she said formally, 'I would like to go to bed.'

He rose too and she tensed, but he swung away from her over to the other side of the room to the sideboard, where he extracted a bottle of whisky and a glass from a carved cupboard.

He gave her an ironic bow as he poured some of the liquid into the glass.

'On your way, *madame*, and sleep sweetly. You won't be interrupted, I give you my word. As you see, I have company for the evening.' He lifted the glass to his lips and drank, then poured some more.

She bit her lip. 'And there is Simone,' some inner demon prompted her to say. 'No doubt you have a great deal to talk about together—old times to discuss.'

He set the glass down with almost frightening deliberation.

'What, in the name of all the devils in hell, do you mean by that?' he said very softly.

'Not a great deal,' she said wearily. 'But it's obvious you have known her for a long time. You must have memories in common—Belle Rivière for one.'

'They are not memories I cherish.' He paused. 'No, *ma mie*, I have nothing to discuss with Simone, and if I had other plans for her—entertainment, I wouldn't need alcohol to stimulate my performance, I promise you. Now take yourself out of my sight,' he added savagely, and she fled.

Alone in the great bed, she tossed restlessly on the unfamiliar mattress while sleep eluded her. Her head throbbed and was answered by a very different ache deep inside her that she tried in vain to stifle. Images kept forcing themselves into her tired mind—images of Philippe waking alone and frightened in the dark—of Blaise and Simone alone together in the firelight downstairs. No matter how indifferent he claimed to be, Simone was a beautiful woman with an air of overt sensuality. But was it merely indifference? His attitude in the past when he had referred to Simone had implied dislike, or even something stronger. Yet hate was supposed to be akin to love or at least desire, and he had made love to herself, quite cold-bloodedly, in order to teach her a lesson.

She shivered in spite of the warmth of the quilt which covered her, and tensed suddenly as she heard the bedroom door open quietly. She closed her eyes and lay motionless, her heart beating quickly and painfully as she heard Blaise moving about. She heard the faint squeak of a cupboard door and guessed he was looking for blankets and covers. Then his footsteps quietly approached the bed and she almost stopped breathing.

'Don't be alarmed, *madame*,' he drawled. 'I only want a pillow. Surely you don't grudge me that much comfort at least?'

Furious with herself for her inept pretence at sleep, she opened her eyes and looked up at him, but he was only a shadowy figure in the darkness of the room.

'Poor Andrée.' The mockery was even more pronounced. 'What an ordeal—to have to share a room with your husband even for one night! And you will be relieved to hear it only will be for one night. Simone tells me she intends to leave first thing in the morning.'

He waited, but she did not answer, and after a moment he laughed softly and moved away.

She lay in the darkness listening to the rustle of his clothes as he undressed, and the protesting creak of the couch as he stretched out on it. It was only when the deep, regular sound of his breathing promised her that he was asleep that she allowed herself the luxury of turning her face into her pillow and crying like an exhausted child.

CHAPTER SEVEN

THE moment Andrea awoke next morning, she knew something was wrong. Everything seemed oddly hushed, and there was hard brilliant light penetrating the curtains.

She pushed back the covers and shivered as the chill air hit her body like a blow. Her eyes went immediately to the couch, but it was unoccupied, the blankets restored to whatever storage place they came from, and the pillow resting once more beside her own on the bed.

She swung her legs to the floor and padded across the room, hugging her arms round her body, but too impatient to see if Gaston's prophecy had come true to stop to put on her dressing gown.

She tugged the curtain aside and gasped at the white world laid out for her inspection. It had snowed in the night and heavily too, and was still snowing now, big silent flakes from a leaden sky which unequivocally promised more to come.

The courtyard, the ruined wing, every building within view was transformed into a fairytale scene of breathtaking loveliness. But even as she gasped with enchantment, Andrea remembered with a sinking sensation in her stomach that Gaston had also predicted that the road to the village would be blocked.

She glanced at her watch, pulling a face when she saw it was nearly time for breakfast. She knew while she was pulling on her clothes that Simone would still be with them. It was impossible that she should have left, considering the present state of the roads and the promise of more snow to come. Andrea could have screamed with vexation. Apart from anything else, she did not think she could stand another night like the one she had just spent.

When she entered the dining room, for a moment she thought it was deserted, and then she saw Philippe kneeling on the window seat, his nose pressed against the panes, his whole body tensed with suppressed excitement. He turned and looked at her, his eyes wide and shining.

'Snow!' he almost gasped, and Andrea realised what a novelty it must seem to a child probably born and reared in the tropics.

She smiled, trying to fall in with his mood, in spite of her own forebodings.

'Isn't it lovely?' she agreed, joining him at the window. 'After breakfast, we'll have such fun. We'll have a fight with snowballs, and I'll see if Gaston can find some timber somewhere to make you a sledge.'

Philippe seemed a little unsure of the exact nature of the delights that were to come his way, but he returned her smile hesitantly and allowed himself to be led to the table, just as Madame Bresson came bustling in with a tray.

Her own view of the weather was more of a lamentation. Gaston, it seemed, had been forced to walk to the village that morning to get the bread. The steep road down was impassable except on foot, and great care was needed even then.

'Great care,' Madame repeated, nodding her head at Andrea as if she suspected her of secret ambitions to become a downhill racer.

In spite of the trek to the village, the *croissants* were still warm and utterly delicious, and Philippe tucked in heartily, aided by a liberal helping of jam supplied by Andrea.

The door swung open again to admit Blaise on a cold draught of air. Snowflakes clung to his hair and the shoulders of his coat, and he pulled the coat off and slung it across the settle so that it could dry in the warmth from the fire before joining them at the table.

He accorded Andrea a brief, unsmiling nod as he passed her hair, and ruffled Philippe's hair until it stood up like a cock's comb. '*Bonjour, mon neveu.*'

It was a carelessly affectionate gesture that should have

prompted a laughing, wriggling protest from most children. Incredulously, Andrea saw Philippe, his eyes enormous with terror, flinch away from his uncle's touch as if it burned him. She saw too that his reaction had not been lost on Blaise, who had gone almost rigid, the scar standing out lividly against the tan of his face.

'*Qu'est-ce que j'ai fait?*' he asked quite gently: 'Is it this that frightens you?' His hand went up and touched his scarred cheek.

Philippe stared down at the cloth, his face crimson. He gave an almost convulsive movement and muttered something unintelligible. For a moment, Blaise stood watching the downbent head, then his face hardened and he strode to his chair, reaching for the coffee pot and splashing some of the scalding brew into his cup.

Andrea felt completely bewildered by the whole incident. Philippe had been shy yesterday, it was true, and more than a little hostile, but it had been directed more at herself, she felt. He had displayed none of today's revulsion towards Blaise at any time that she had seen. Could a child be so affected by a minor disfigurement such as a scarred face? She herself hardly noticed it any more, but she knew that Blaise was still deeply self-conscious and sensitive about it, and that Philippe's reaction had been the last thing he needed. Or could it be simply a child's angry response to the change in guardianship over which he, presumably, had not been consulted? Was he simply showing Blaise that he did not want to be parted from Simone? If so, and Andrea was not even convinced it was the case, he could not have chosen a more unfortunate manner of making his feelings known.

She began to talk almost at random, filling the silence with words, telling Philippe about snowy days she remembered from her childhood—the giant snowman she and Clare had once made and how angry Uncle Max had been when he found it adorned by his best silk evening scarf. The feeling of tension in the room was almost tangible, and her ripple of chatter and anecdote seemed just to spend itself against it.

And into the middle of it all came Simone, exotically

wrapped in a silk kimono hand-embroidered with great pale flowers, artistically hiding a yawn behind one manicured hand and apologising with a smile for her lateness. It was too much to hope that she would not notice the atmosphere in the room, and equally useless, Andrea discovered helplessly, to hope that she would refrain from comment.

'*Qu'est-ce qui se passe?*' Simone bit delicately into a *croissant*, her intent gaze travelling from Philippe's flushed face to his uncle's coldly saturnine expression. The little boy's colour became even deeper and he hung his head, reducing the *croissant* on his plate to a pile of crumbs with quick, nervous movements of his fingers.

'*Oh, mon dieu!*' Simone clapped her fingers to her lips. 'Oh, Blaise, I'm so sorry. He's said something, hasn't he—about your face? Philippe, *mon petit*, that was not kind. I warned you that you must learn to hide your feelings ...'

'Let it rest.' Blaise's voice crackled with ice. 'The child should not be blamed. Why should he succeed where his elders fail?'

But Simone did not take the hint. She turned back to Philippe and began to direct a flow of gentle remonstrance towards him. Oh God, Andrea thought despairingly, why doesn't she shut up? Can't she see she's just making everything worse?

It did not altogether surprise her that after a few minutes, Blaise pushed back his chair and strode out of the room, banging the door behind him.

Simone sank back into her chair with an exaggerated sigh. 'What a disaster,' she remarked to the room at large. 'One had hoped that by this time Blaise would have accustomed himself to his affliction.'

'If you thought that, I wonder you found it neccessary to warn Philippe about it in advance.' Andrea found she was shaking with temper inside, but she managed to keep her voice equable.

Simone lifted her eyebrows. 'But I had to say something,' she pointed out. 'Philippe is in a highly nervous state. If I had not prepared him, he might have suffered a complete *crise.* It is not pretty to see, you admit—Blaise's face. When one remembers how he was before . . .'

'But I don't,' Andrea pointed out, then realised her mistake.

That cat's smile peeped again. 'Of course not,' Simone said silkily. 'It must have been a very brief courtship—perhaps love at first sight, *hein*?'

'Something like that,' Andrea managed to return coolly.

'You have a saying—do you not—that marriage in haste leads later to repentance.'

Andrea forced a smile. 'Again—something like that. We have another saying—that we'll have to keep our fingers crossed.'

'But your fingers are not crossed,' observed a small voice at her side.

'Now they are.' Andrea extended her hand with a swift smile.

Philippe studied them with a little frown. 'Rose-Emilie used to do that to send away evil spirits,' he remarked. 'Are you sending away evil spirits, *ma tante*?'

It was the first time he had acknowledged the new relationship that existed between them and Andrea's heart gave a little leap.

'Who is Rose-Emilie?' she asked.

'*Ma bonne.* She lived with us at Belle Rivière and looked after me. She used to tell me stories about the spirits of the forest—stories about Baron Samedi and the goddess Erzulie. They were good stories,' he added rather doubtfully. 'But sometimes they made me frightened.'

'I'm not surprised.' Andrea turned to Simone. 'Did you know that all this was going on?'

Simone shrugged idly. 'In other circumstances, Philippe would have grown to manhood on the island,' she said. 'Voodoo is part of the islanders' way of life. He would have accustomed himself in time.'

Oh, would he? Andrea thought silently. She looked down at Philippe. 'Go and put on a warm jersey, *mon petit*,' she urged gently. 'Then you can go out and play.'

It did not take Philippe more than a few moments to discover the joys of snowballing. His first direct hit on Andrea was greeted with a gleeful whoop that delighted her. For the first time, he had begun to sound and behave like an ordinary little boy, she thought.

In the middle of it all, she heard someone tapping on a window and looked up to see Alan peering down at them. She waved at him cheerfully, and made a beckoning gesture, almost without thinking. He vanished with alacrity, obviously intent on joining them, and Andrea felt a pang of compunction. Blaise had already made it clear that he disapproved of her seeing too much of her compatriot. Would it annoy him that she had invited Alan down to join the snowball fight?

It was too late now to regret her impulse. Alan was already emerging from the gatehouse, shrugging himself into an ancient combat jacket, his eyes beaming behind his glasses.

'Whom have we here?' he asked, shaking the hand Philippe extended to him with due solemnity.

'My husband's ward. He's come to live with us.' Andrea tried to keep her tone noncommittal.

'Lucky lad.' Alan looked round approvingly. 'Paradise for kids, this place.'

'Yes.' Andrea felt subdued suddenly. 'Yes, I suppose it is.'

And one day it will all belong to him. Did Philippe know that? she wondered. And did Simone know it too? She gave herself a little mental shake. Of them all, she had to be the least concerned. She would not be here after all, to see Philippe come into his inheritance. And once her marriage was annulled, or a divorce was arranged, Simone's future role in all this would cease to concern her too. She had to remember this, to remember she was only there on sufferance, an unwilling partner in a marriage of convenience. Otherwise she was in grave danger of finding herself emotionally broken on the reefs of Blaise's indifference.

Forcing herself to an almost desperate gaiety, she seized

a handful of snow and flung it at Alan, and within seconds the snow fight was on again, its pace even faster and more furious than before.

After a while, Andrea noticed that Philippe had begun to flag and guessed that he was not used to this type of strenuous exercise, so she suggested they should go round to the stable block and see if they could find Gaston.

She had wondered if the little boy would be nervous of horses, but he displayed no fear at all, and began feeding them handfuls of oats. Gaston was in the workshop which doubled as a tack room just off the main block, carefully applying a coat of fresh varnish to a large old-fashioned toboggan. Andrea exclaimed with delight and he grinned at her, while his fingers worked deftly. From his mumbled remarks, she gathered it had once been the plaything of Blaise and his brother, and she sighed inwardly as she visualised the two children playing together, with no premonitions of the tragedy and bitterness future years were to bring.

She heard a muted gasp at her side and looked down to see Philippe had come to join them.

'*Pour moi?*' He pointed almost disbelievingly at the toboggan and Andrea turned reassuringly.

'All for you,' she told him.

He drew a deep contented breath and a small cold hand crept into hers.

'It has not taken you long to find the way to Philippe's heart, Andrée.' Simone's voice was mocking as she stood in the doorway behind them. Andrea gave her a constrained smile, angry with herself for the instinctive jump she had given at the first sound of Simone's voice. She really had the noiseless approach down to a fine art, she thought crossly.

Simone strolled forward. She was wearing a trouser suit in a deep shade of red which managed to be vivid without being garish. The jacket had a large hood trimmed with white fur, and this was drawn up to frame her face becomingly. Alan was staring at her with his jaw dropping and Andrea could willingly have kicked him on the ankle.

Simone smiled around her. 'What a charming scene,' she remarked. 'A cosy family party—except that I do not think I have ever met you before, *monsieur.* Won't you introduce us, Andrée?'

Andrea complied with gritted teeth, registering as she knew she was intended to do that Simone apparently considered herself one of the family.

Simone was all charm, questioning Alan with apparently genuine interest on the nature of his researches, and listening to his replies with a rapt attention which would have flattered a man with twice Alan's sophistication. Perched elegantly on the corner of a work-bench, toying idly with an enormous screwdriver against which her hands looked amazingly small and fragile, Simone was an enchanting picture.

It was no wonder Philippe was bewitched, Andrea thought ruefully. He had let her hand go as the other girl had appeared, and was standing a few feet away with his head bent. The healthy flush that snowballing had engendered had faded, and he looked small and sallow again. Andrea was conscious of a sudden impulse to pick him up in her arms and hug him soundly, but she deliberately repressed it. It was all too likely that he would rebuff her, she thought, and that would give satisfaction to no one but Simone. She would just have to make haste slowly where Philippe was concerned.

Simone gave a little exaggerated start and clapped her hand to her mouth. 'But I forget everything!' Her smile embraced them all. 'Clothilde has made hot chocolate *pour tout le monde.* It will be cold if we do not go soon.' She swung herself lightly to the floor and tucked her arm through Alan's. 'You must come too, *monsieur.* If you have never tasted Clothilde's chocolate, then you have missed an unforgettable experience, *je vous assure.*'

She led him out of the tack room and back towards the chateau, leaving Andrea to follow somewhat dazedly with Philippe, wondering exactly who was the hostess and who the guest.

The chocolate was quite delicious, dark and sweet and topped with a swirl of cream, and Madame Bresson had made some small cakes, tasting of almond and still warm from the oven, to accompany it. Alan's eyes positively glistened when he saw them and he needed very little urging to help himself, which confirmed a lot of Andrea's suspicions about the austerity of his usual diet. She wondered if Blaise could be persuaded to invite him to dinner at the chateau occasionally, a train of thought which came to an abrupt halt with Blaise's own arrival. He was obviously in an irritable mood, but whether this was a hangover from the little scene at breakfast or caused by something that had happened during his morning's work, she had no means of knowing. One thing was certain. Blaise took one look at Alan and his slight frown deepened to thunder. Fortunately Alan himself seemed unaware of the paucity of his welcome from his host, or at least pretended not to notice, but the chocolate and cakes seemed to turn to ashes in Andrea's mouth.

She was not in the least surprised when after a few minutes, Alan announced that he had to get back to his work and got up, ready to depart, to Philippe's open disappointment.

'But my toboggan,' he protested through a mouthful of cake. 'You said you would show me how to ride it.'

'So I will,' Alan returned good-naturedly. 'But not today. The varnish won't be dry yet, for one thing. Don't worry,' he added, as Philippe's bottom lip began to jut stormily. 'The snow will be with us for days yet.'

Andrea's heart sank at his words. As long as the snow remained, so, it seemed, would Simone. She was still thoughtful when she returned to the dining room after showing Alan to the door—a task, she noticed ironically, that Simone did not volunteer for. As she resumed her seat, she encountered a chillingly bleak look from her husband.

'I thought I had made it clear that while I may tolerate that young man as a tenant, it does not mean I wish to entertain him as a guest.'

Andrea's eyes flashed indignantly, but before she could answer, Simone had interrupted.

'*Mon dieu!*' She looked from Blaise's granite-like face to Andrea's flushed cheeks. 'I see I have been indiscreet. Why did you not warn me, Andrée, that Blaise would be angry? But you must not blame your wife, *mon cher*. I invited her young Englishman to have chocolate with us. He is *très charmant*,' she added with an air of almost childlike candour. 'I do not blame you for having a fondness for him.'

'But I don't,' Andrea began heatedly, then subsided, suddenly wary. She was conscious that no matter what she said, she would not emerge from the exchange with credit. Simone had managed to imply that she had some need to behave with discretion where Alan was concerned. Any protest she made after that was bound to sound either feeble, or altogether too vehement, as if she really did have something to hide. She picked up her cup and drank, but the chocolate was tepid, and the morning destroyed for her. Foolishly, she wanted to cry.

The next three days dragged past. Each morning as she reluctantly opened her eyes, Andrea found herself praying that some miracle might have occurred during the night, and that there might have been a swift thaw, but each morning as she drew back the curtains it was the same uncompromisingly white world she looked out on.

The snow began to seem like an enemy, threatening and beautiful, no matter how many times she told herself she was being ridiculous. She forced herself to share Philippe's pleasure in it, joining in the daily snowball fights, helping him to build snowmen and animals which stood around the courtyard like absurd sentinels. Sometimes they went for long walks together, but Andrea did not fool herself that she was drawing any closer to the child, or making headway in establishing a relationship with him. More often than not they walked in silence, occasionally exchanging a guarded smile. Any tentative questions Andrea put to him about his life at Belle Rivière or later with

Simone were greeted by blank looks and monosyllabic replies, and she accepted this and forbore to ask again.

She was only too aware that when they returned home it was Simone he looked for eagerly, running to show her any treasures he had collected on their walk—a glossy bird's wing, an unusual pebble, a clump of flowers discovered in a sheltered corner.

Blaise he never went near. There was tension whenever the two of them were in the room together. At mealtimes, Philippe sat hunched and silent in his chair, his eyes fixed on his plate. And there was no question of being able to explain his behaviour away by the fact that he responded better to women. Philippe was constantly to be found in Gaston's company, running countless small errands, carrying in logs. He spent part of every day in the gatehouse too, listening entranced to long-ago tales of Vercingetorix the Gaul and his guerrilla war against the Romans, which he re-enacted with garbled enthusiasm for a bored Simone in the evenings.

The evenings, Andrea thought, were the worst of all. She could keep herself occupied during the day, taking more and more of the housekeeping reins into her hands and learning to cope with the intricacies of Madame Bresson's kitchen range. During the afternoons, Madame drew her high-backed chair close to the fire and got on with her lacemaking. Andrea did not ask to be given lessons—she knew that the traditional patterns evolving under Madame's flying bobbins were a closely guarded secret—but it was peaceful to sit in the warm, homely kitchen watching the unassuming expertise with which Madame performed her craft.

But in the evenings, there were several empty hours to be got through between the completion of dinner and the time when she could decently excuse herself and go up to her room. She found a pile of sheets in a cupboard and set herself to patching them, finding an odd escape in the total mindlessness of the occupation.

When she did get to her room, all she could do was lie

in the darkness, waiting endlessly for the moment when the door would open.

Each night she made up the bed on the couch for Blaise, smoothing the pillow and arranging the covers to her own satisfaction. And each night she lay still, trying to control the evenness of her breathing when he came into the room, oddly terrified that he would know of her wakefulness. But he never spoke or gave the slightest sign he was even aware of her presence, and she knew as she dropped at last into an uneasy sleep that however early she woke the following morning, he would already be gone.

As she brushed her hair and tied it back, she was aware of shadows beneath her eyes and a new wistfulness around her mouth. The girl who had come so recklessly to Auvergne to rescue her cousin seemed a million miles away. She gave a swift impatient sigh and turned away from the mirror, her slenderness emphasised by the black corded jeans and matching ribbed sweater she was wearing.

As she descended the stairs, she wondered what creation Simone would be wearing that day, and found herself smiling faintly. It was almost as if Simone had had advance warning that she would be snowed up at the chateau perhaps for days, and had come prepared with a wardrobe that would not have been out of place on a jet set winter sports holiday. At least, her constant changes of clothes gave her an occupation of sorts, Andrea thought, and grimaced at her own malice. Certainly there was little else for Simone to do. She was not interested in any of the books at the chateau, and she made no effort to conceal her annoyance that there was no form of canned entertainment. Almost in desperation, Andrea had unearthed an elderly chessboard from the depths of the sideboard, but chess was not to Simone's taste either.

She seemed to prefer to spend her time in animated and totally one-sided conversations with Blaise, ignoring Andrea completely as soon as Philippe had left them for the night. Andrea soon found she could not follow half of what the other girl was saying, and guessing that this was what Simone intended, gave up the struggle and concentrated on her needlework instead.

But at least she was spared her company at breakfast these days, Andrea thought as she opened the dining room door. Simone now partook of coffee and rolls in her room, and often didn't come downstairs until it was nearly lunchtime.

She was quite unprepared for the scene which met her eyes. Philippe looking small and defensive was backed against the window seat. His eyes were wide and scared as he stared up at Blaise who was towering over him, obviously angry. As Andrea appeared in the doorway, he gave a little choked cry and ran to her side. Blaise swung round, his hands resting on his hips, and confronted the pair of them.

'How fortunate that my nephew has a refuge in you, *madame*.' His dark face was openly sneering as he looked at them. 'Your timely appearance has probably saved him from a good hiding.'

'What has he done?' Andrea put a hand on Philippe's shoulder and felt it trembling.

'Borrowed some of Gaston's tools and failed to return them. Now Gaston needs them urgently for some jobs he wishes to do, and the tools cannot be found anywhere.'

'Oh, Philippe.' Andrea put her hand under his chin. 'That was naughty. If you borrow something, you must return it. Where are the tools? We'll take them back to Gaston.'

Philippe's lip quivered as he looked up at her. 'I—have not got them.'

'Then where are they?'

The child paused, then shrugged. 'I did return them,' he said eventually in a low voice. 'They must be there. Gaston must be lying.'

'There is only one liar in this room,' Blaise interjected coldly.

'Oh, please.' Andrea put up an appealing hand. 'That isn't going to help.'

'Then what is?' he demanded, his face hard and set.

'You think you will persuade him to tell the truth? I have already tried persuasion, *madame*, and it does not work. If you can convince him that it is not to his advantage to add to his guilt by lying about his misdemeanour, then you will have done us both a service.'

Andrea groaned inwardly, then knelt down beside Philippe.

'You did borrow the tools?' she began, and he nodded.

'I was a sculptor,' he explained simply. 'I made a statue of Vercingetorix from a block of snow.'

'I see.' Andrea sat back on her heels. 'Then what did you do? Did you leave the tools in the snow?'

'No!' The rebuttal was indignant. 'Gaston has told me many times that such things must be cared for. I—I took them back,' he added with obvious hesitation.

'Then they must be there,' Andrea tried to sound cheerful. 'Perhaps you just put them in the wrong place . . .'

'Gaston and I have both searched,' Blaise said abruptly. 'There is no sign of any of them. The truth is Philippe has left them out in the snow and is afraid to confess his fault.'

Sudden hot colour rose under Philippe's skin. 'I am not afraid.' His voice was shrill. 'It is you who is the coward, Monsieur la Cicatrice. You let my father die. I hate you!'

He whipped around, freeing himself from Andrea's detaining hand and was gone, the door banging stormily behind him.

Andrea looked up at Blaise, her own eyes wide with astonishment, and saw that he was white to the lips, the scar standing out in livid contrast. He saw her questioning gaze and his own eyes narrowed.

'What do you want me to say?' he asked. 'Do you want me to deny what he says? I cannot. My brother died because I failed to rescue him. If his son wishes to brand me as a coward then that is something else that I must learn to live with—along with this.' His hand went up and touched his disfigured cheek.

Andrea scrambled to her feet. 'Philippe says you let his father die. You say that you failed to rescue him. There's a world of difference between the two stories.'

'A difference in emphasis, perhaps.' He stared past her. His face might have been carved out of stone. 'Jean-Paul is no less dead, however.'

'Blaise, how did it happen? Jean-Paul's death—your face—everything?'

For a long moment, she thought he was going to ignore her questions and walk past her out of the room into this private hell of his own making, but after a while he gave a short sigh and his eyes seemed to register her again.

'Jean-Paul died in the fire that destroyed Belle Rivière,' he said colourlessly. 'He believed—God alone knows why—that Philippe was still in the house. He broke free from us—he was like a mad thing—and ran back into the burning building. I went after him. I was shouting to him—I could see him just ahead of me. I could have sworn he heard me and was turning to come back, when there was some kind of an explosion. The next thing I remember is some of the plantation workers dragging me out of some rubble and seeing their faces when they looked at mine. They told me later that no trace of my brother had been found. I think this was to spare me.'

He turned away and walked over to the window, standing with his back to her, looking out.

'I can sympathise with Philippe,' he said after a pause. 'Jean-Paul was loved by everyone who knew him. I can understand why Philippe cannot comprehend why his father was taken, and I was left. I have wondered the same thing myself.' He thrust his hands into his pockets. 'I understand too why he shrinks from the sight of my face. Every time he sees me, I must remind him of Jean-Paul and how he died.'

'But he was scarcely more than a baby when it happened.' Andrea's hands clenched helplessly at her sides.

'*C'est vrai.* But if one has a strong enough motive, one can sow the seeds of memory even in the mind of a child as young as Philippe.'

A shiver ran through her body. She wanted desperately

to ask. 'And your fiancée? What of her?' But the words would not be uttered.

Other things, however, had to be said.

'You've got to stop blaming yourself,' she said, very quickly before her courage melted away. 'There was nothing more you could have done.'

He was silent for so long she thought he had not heard what she said, then he said quietly, 'That is what I have tried to tell myself, but I know it is not the truth. I could have stopped the whole thing at the outset. It need never have happened.'

Andrea shook her head bewilderedly. What was he referring to—the fire—Jean-Paul's death?

She walked across the room to his side, and put her hand on his arm, making him turn and look down at her. His eyes were shuttered and enigmatic, his mouth set in grim lines.

'Don't concern yourself for me, *ma mie*,' he advised her brusquely. 'There are many more deserving cases for your charity than myself.'

'It's not a question of charity,' she denied stormily. 'And how can I help being concerned? I'm a human being after all, even though I know I'm just a pawn to you in this weird chess game you seem to be playing with your conscience. But I have feelings and emotions too. I'm not an automaton, Blaise, and I can't make myself into one for you.'

Her voice was shaking uncontrollably as she broke off. His face swam at her as she stared up at him with tear-dimmed eyes, then obeying an impulse she barely understood, she reached up and pressed her lips for one warm, fleeting instant to the scar on his cheek. For a moment he was rigid, then with a small harsh sound he pulled her into his arms and sought her mouth with his. Her lips parted for him instinctively, her body moulding itself breathlessly against the long, hard length of his. His kiss was as gentle as a snowflake and at the same time, in some magical way, as fierce as the storm wind. At last he let her go, standing looking down into her face with eyes that burned into hers while his hands moved on her body with a demand that became ever more urgent until at last with an incoherent murmur she offered him her mouth again.

It was the sound of the dining room door softly closing that brought them back to reality. Andrea heard Blaise curse softly under his breath as he released her. She left the strength of his arms with a reluctance she did not bother to disguise.

'I suppose that was Madame Bresson with our breakfast,' she said with a slight catch in her voice.

'Reminding us that we can only satisfy one hunger at a time, *hein*?' He was smiling as he spoke, but there was a warm, sensual intensity in his gaze that sent the blood racing giddily through her veins. She returned his smile, her shining eyes, parted lips and faintly flushed cheeks an unconscious provocation.

'*Sacre dieu!*' he breathed, and took a step towards her, checking as the dining room door swung open again to admit Madame Bresson with a tray.

Andrea expected at the least a knowing glance from the housekeeper's dark eyes as she placed the food on the table, but Madame's face merely wore its usual amiable expression, and she gave no sign of her awareness of the scene she had interrupted only minutes before.

She was angry to find her hand shaking as she picked up the coffee pot, and knew that her tremulousness was not lost on Blaise. To mask her embarrassment, she turned to Madame, asking about Philippe's whereabouts in an unwontedly sharp tone. Madame looked surprised but answered that she had seen *le petit* making for the gatehouse.

'Monsieur Alan will feed him, *madame*, have no fear,' she added with a broad smile and took her departure.

It was not an easy meal to get through. Andrea was conscious of nothing but the proximity of the man who sat just across the table from her. She was bewildered by the force of her own emotions and desires, and a little frightened too. At the back of her mind lurked the fear that by yielding to him so completely she was providing him with another opportunity to torment her as cruelly as he had done on their wedding night. The warm bread and fragrant coffee tasted like stale crusts and water as she remembered the humiliation she had suffered at his hands. Yet at the same time she sensed a difference in his attitude towards her. There had been a tenderness, almost a pleading in his kisses, which had been absent before, as if he too was vulnerable now.

'Relax, *ma mie.*' Blaise's voice came sardonically to her, and she started, spilling some of her coffee on to the linen cloth. 'I won't force my animal lusts on you at the breakfast table, I promise you. I prefer to wait for a time when we are truly alone and safe from interruptions.'

'I didn't—I mean I wasn't ...' She was blushing fierily, and it didn't help at all that he was laughing at her.

'*Ma pauvre* Andrée.' He glanced at his watch and rose to his feet. 'It is unkind to tease you, but quite irresistible, believe me. Now I must go. I have meetings this morning and later this afternoon, so I shall not be here for lunch. However'— and his voice took on a drawl—'I shall return in time for dinner—tonight.'

In the short silence that followed, Andrea heard herself swallow quite deafeningly.

He came slowly round the table to her, and she rose too, pushing her chair back and leaning slightly on the edge of the table, conscious suddenly that she could not trust her legs to support her unaided.

He lifted her palm to his lips, pressing his mouth against the softness of her palm as he had done on the night he had given her the betrothal ring. His smile gleamed again as he looked at her.

'Don't be frightened, *ma belle.* I don't always behave like a brute, you know.'

'I don't think of you as a brute,' she answered him unevenly.

He lifted one brow mockingly. 'No? Then you must be very forgiving.'

He slid a hand under the smooth fall of her hair and began to stroke the nape of her neck very gently with his fingertips.

'Tonight, Andrée,' his voice sank to a whisper. 'Tonight I will show you just how gentle I can be. *Soit*?'

'*Soit*,' she managed.

The hand clasping her neck suddenly compelled her towards him. He bent, pulling aside the high collar of her sweater, and kissing the soft curve of her throat. His mouth had left a mark on her flesh when he eventually raised his head.

'Think of me today,' he said quietly, and left her.

Alone, Andrea sank down on to her chair, and tried to collect her thoughts. Think of him! She would be fortunate if she managed to think of anything else. Yet, no matter how high the springs of feeling he had released within her might be bubbling, the fact remained that a number of problems still confronted her, and the main one of these was undoubtedly Philippe. What lasting happiness could she hope for with Blaise while he still carried this burden of guilt for his brother's death? Somehow, if they were to have any chance at all, she would have to reconcile Philippe with his uncle, include the child in their own love and joy. It surely wasn't such an impossible task? Whatever influences might have been brought to bear on Philippe could surely be counteracted? She felt herself shiver slightly. He was such a suggestible child, and stories of black magic and death had been told to him since babyhood. Was she capable of convincing him that love and life and hope still existed? It wouldn't be easy—she knew that.

For a moment, she wondered idly why Simone had fought so hard to obtain possession of the child. In spite of the fact that she still insisted on putting him to bed each night, she took very little interest in him otherwise, although it was obvious that Philippe adored her.

She was glad, in a way, to know that when he had run away today, he had gone to Alan, and not to Simone. Perhaps it was a hopeful sign that he had accepted the fact that the chains which bound him to her had to be broken.

Andrea sighed. It was such a hard lesson for a small boy to learn. But perhaps Philippe was fortunate in learning so early in his life how bleak it could be to worship at an empty shrine. If Simone had been a different personality—warm and affectionate, then Philippe's parting from her might have been heartrending indeed.

She got up. One thing was certain. He couldn't spend all day with Alan, who would be wanting to work. She would go and collect him, saying nothing of the scene before breakfast, and they would help feed the horses before they went on their walk. It was daily rituals like these that childhood was made of, she thought. Philippe might never give her the devotion he apparently accorded Simone, but at least she could come to represent security in his uncertain little world.

She went out of the dining room, hugging her arms across herself in the chill air of the great hall. The massive door swung open to admit Gaston carrying a great basket of logs. His round eyes twinkled at her and his grin threatened to split his face in half.

'*Regardez, madame.*' He gestured hugely back towards where he had come from. '*Le vent est au degel.* The wind is bringing us a thaw. Soon the snow will melt and disappear.'

'Will it?' Andrea tried to return his smile, but an uncontrollable feeling of apprehension gripped her.

The thaw had come at last, perhaps, but might it not already be too late?

CHAPTER EIGHT

ANDREA had to knock quite loudly on the gatehouse door before Alan's feet could be heard descending the stairs. He pulled the door open.

'He's asleep,' he said without preamble. He took off his glasses and rubbed his eyes. 'I thought you'd be coming.'

'Is he all right?' she stared at him, suddenly anxious.

'That depends on your interpretation of all right.' He stool back to allow her to precede him up the stairs. 'That—in case you hadn't noticed—is one mixed-up kid.'

'I had noticed,' she said in a low voice.

Philippe was lying on the camp bed in the corner, his face streaked with tears. His breathing was slow and rhythmical, and his face blank and smoothed out by slumber.

'He's been dreaming.' Alan shook his little kettle to assess the amount of water it held, then placed it on the stove and applied a light to the gas jet. 'Bad dreams. I thought I'd have to wake him up again. Whatever prompted you to tell him the story of the tower and Marie-Denise?'

'I didn't,' she denied indignantly. 'I wouldn't be so stupid.'

'That's what I felt, but I couldn't be sure.' He was silent for a moment. 'Then what about that housekeeper woman—Clothilde, is it?'

'She wouldn't either.' Andrea shook her head firmly. 'I think she believes it's bad luck even to mention the story.'

Alan busied himself with tea-making. As he passed a steaming mug to her, he said almost idly,

'You do know he thinks his uncle is trying to kill him?'

Andrea almost dropped the tea. Her eyes widened endlessly as she looked up at him. 'What are you saying?'

'It's true.' He tasted his brew and added more sugar, stirring it reflectively. 'For some reason Philippe has got it fixed in his head that Marie-Denise's husband had a scar on his cheek and that his uncle—your husband—is his ancestor come back to life again. And he is also convinced that history is going to repeat itself, and that's why he's been put in that tower room.' He took a gulp of tea and sat down. 'He falls asleep every time he comes, poor kid. I don't think he gets much sleep at nights, somehow—probably too afraid. A couple of times when he's been here he's been restless—muttering things. It took me a while to figure out what he was saying and then I realised he was muttering "*La Cicatrice*" over and over again.'

'That's what he called Blaise earlier,' Andrea said mechanically, her mind whirring. She clasped her hands around the mug, comforted by the warmth of the tea against the sudden chill which had invaded her being.

'Yes, I'd gathered there'd been a row.' Alan looked at her curiously. 'He arrived in quite a state—crying, almost hysterical. It took me a while to calm him down, and I guessed there must have been some kind of crisis.'

'It was all rather silly,' Andrea said wearily. 'Philippe had borrowed some of Gaston's tools and apparently lost them. Blaise took him to task, quite justifiably, and got angry when he refused to admit he'd done wrong.'

Alan looked at her narrowly. 'But all this fuss over a small incident like that?'

After a pause, she shook her head. 'No,' she admitted. 'There's been—tension between them ever since Philippe arrived. He's terrified of Blaise, and he shows it. But I had no idea that this was the reason.' She looked up at Alan anxiously. 'I—I feel responsible to some extent. It was my idea to put Philippe in the tower rooms, after all. I didn't realise the story of Marie-Denise would be known to him. It's not the sort of thing you tell a young child, after all.'

'Especially not one as impressionable as Philippe,' Alan agreed. 'And where has he got the idea from that Marie-Denise's husband had a scarred face?'

Andrea lifted her shoulders resignedly. 'I've no idea,' she confessed. 'I didn't even know that myself.'

'Of course you didn't.' Alan's tone was dry. 'There's not a word of truth in it.'

For a moment she was too taken aback to speak, then she said slowly. 'But that's—cruel. Cruel on them both.'

'Indeed it is.' Alan drained his mug of tea and set it down. 'Someone's out to make mischief. Who that is, and why, you're probably in a better position to know than I am.' He looked down at the floor. 'From things Philippe has let drop, I gather there's been some hassle over his guardianship.'

'Yes,' she said in a low voice. 'You've met Mademoiselle Delatour—Simone. She is Philippe's aunt on his mother's side. She was very disappointed not to be awarded custody, and was prepared, I think, to do legal battle over Jean-Paul Levallier's will.'

'Hm.' Alan pushed his hands through his hair. 'She's a gorgeous bird, but not altogether my idea of a succourer of orphans. What's in it for her?'

Andrea stared at him. 'Why, nothing. There was a plantation called Belle Rivière, and a house, but they've both gone now, and the land has been leased to the government. Philippe has nothing to come from that, although he is Blaise's heir.'

'Until Monsieur Levallier has a son of his own.'

For a moment she did not comprehend his meaning, then when realisation dawned, the colour swept into her face.

'Yes—of course,' she said lamely, trying to master her composure. She moistened her lips. 'It's because of Belle Rivière that Philippe is so antagonistic towards Blaise. There was a fire there, you see, and Jean-Paul, Philippe's father, was killed in it. Blaise blames himself for this same reason, and the terrible thing is Philippe blames him too, quite openly. Somehow he's got hold of a distorted version of the facts . . .'

'And not for the first time either,' Alan pointed out. He was silent for a moment, 'It's the old *Hamlet* theme all over again—destroying someone by pouring poison into their ear. Oh, not literally, of course. But the destruction of a child's whole personality and trust comes as near murder as need be.'

Even as he spoke, Philippe turned on his side and opened his eyes, muttering something. Alan moved over to him.

'*Holà, mon gars*,' he said cheerfully. 'Here is your aunt come to collect you.'

Philippe sat up, hugging his knees. His glance travelled past Alan to Andrea and became intent.

'Is my uncle still angry?' he asked in a small voice.

'I think that he's more hurt than anything else.' Andrea forced her voice to remain calm and even, in spite of the nightmare of doubts and apprehensions that Alan's words had aroused in her. 'How could you have said such a thing to him, Philippe?'

The child shrugged sullenly and looked at the floor. 'It is the truth,' he said.

Andrea sighed inwardly, but there seemed little point in continuing the discussion which could easily degenerate into a series of contradictions, achieving nothing.

She put out her hand encouragingly. 'Come along, *chéri*. Delphine will think you have deserted her if you don't take her some titbits.'

He hesitated for a moment, and she thought he was going to refuse to accompany her, and that she was part of his general mistrust of everyone and everything at the chateau, but with a last shrug, he climbed off the bed and took her hand.

As they emerged into the courtyard and began to make their way round to the stables, she said gently, 'Philippe, would you rather sleep in a different room?'

He made no reply, and when she glanced down she saw him gazing up at her with wide, startled eyes. She went quietly on: 'Because there are plenty of other rooms, you know, in the main part of the house. You may choose one, if you wish.'

He swallowed nervously, then shook his head.

'You're sure?' she asked. 'If you were in the house, you would be nearer to me—if you needed anything in the night. Although,' she added hastily, 'if you called out now, I would hear you. The tower isn't very far from our—my room.'

He nodded thoughtfully, and sent her a sidelong glance. '*Merci, madame*. I think, however, that I will remain where I am,' he said with a touchingly quaint formality.

She gave him an impulsive hug, conscious of a swift feeling of relief. Whatever terrors Philippe possessed, he seemed to be in control of them at the moment. Surely she could build on that.

'That's the spirit, *mon brave*.' She smiled gaily down at him.

Gaston was standing in the doorway to the stable block, his face set in unusually grim lines. As soon as he set eyes on Philippe, he broke into a flood of excitable French, gesturing with unmistakable anger.

Andrea groaned inwardly. 'What is missing now, Gaston?' she asked.

'*Rien, madame*—but only see for yourself.' He stood aside so that she could see what lay on the floor behind him.

The splintered heap of wood was scarcely recognisable as the sledge that Gaston had laboured over with such care to renovate for Philippe only a few days earlier. A hammer lay on top of the mass of splinters, as if the perpetrator had flung it down, too tired to persist in any more destruction.

Andrea made a small shocked sound and turned to Philippe. He stood like a statue, staring at the wrecked sledge, and she felt his hand begin to tremble in hers.

'Why, Philippe?' Uncaring of the mess on the stone floor, she knelt, pulling him round to face her. 'Because it belonged to your uncle Blaise? It also belonged to your papa, you know. They shared it, and now it has gone for ever. Was that what you wanted?'

There were two brilliant spots of colour in the child's cheeks. His lips compressed tightly, he tore himself free of her and ran off as if he was being pursued by avenging Furies.

Gaston picked up the hammer with a sorrowful air.

'See, *madame*? This is the hammer that was missing. And where are the other implements, one asks oneself? What will he do with them? *Vraiment*, I think Monsieur Philippe is possessed by a devil!'

A devil of despair, perhaps, Andrea thought, as she

turned away shakily. She was more disturbed by this incident than by anything that had gone before. This—this was violence, uncontrolled and dangerous, and she could only guess at the depth of emotion that had driven the child to such an act. It was almost unbelievable that he could have done such a thing. He had loved that sledge, and played eagerly on it as soon as he had been given permission, had behaved, in fact, like the child he was, instead of the fledgling adult role which circumstances seemed to have forced him into.

She wondered, half-distractedly, if she ought to go after him. She had never felt so totally at a loss, needing a wisdom that was beyond her years and experience. She'd had so little to do with young children, and Philippe was still a stranger to her.

And there was not even Blaise to consult, she remembered hopelessly. There were tears pricking at her eyelids as she walked blindly back into the chateau. She shut the great door and leaned her back against it for a moment, feeling the ancient strength of the timbers. The reminder of the storms and crises they must have weathered over the years gave her a sort of comfort.

'Are you ill?'

Opening her eyes almost dazedly, she saw Simone standing on the bottom stair, watching her. She held a cigarette, flicking the ash away with an abrupt, nervous gesture which seemed somehow out of character, Andrea thought. Simone was elegant—measured in everything she did.

'No, I'm fine,' she replied with an immense effort to sound normal.

Simone's eyes were frankly speculative. '*Eh bien.* And where is Philippe? I have been trying to teach him to read, and it is time for his lesson.'

Andrea pushed her hair back wearily. 'I—I'm not sure. Playing somewhere, I think.'

The lie rose instinctively to her lips, prompted by some indefinable certainty that Simone should not know what had happened.

'Playing or sulking?' Simone's faint smile held more than a trace of malice. 'You forget, *ma chère*, how well I know him. He is a strange child,' she added meditatively. 'Given to odd moods, capable of strong hatreds and much bitterness. My sister was not like that—nor was his father Jean-Paul. Perhaps he resembles his uncle Blaise, in whom one can also detect much bitterness. I do not envy you your life with either of them.'

Andrea pressed her fingers against her eyes. Her voice seemed to come from a long way away. 'What are you playing at, Simone?'

She was horrified as soon as she had spoken, unknowing where the words had come from.

Simone's dark eyes were as hard as agates. 'No game, *ma chère* Andrée, believe me. I am merely trying to make you see sense at last. No matter what Blaise may have told you, Philippe is really better off with me. I can—handle him.' Her smile, suddenly, was full of charm and persuasion, her eyes veiled by her long lashes. 'Won't you speak to Blaise for me—please, Andrée? It is ridiculous for us to be at odds in this matter. Philippe belongs with me—he is happy with me. When I go, there will be nothing but trouble for you.'

'You're very convincing,' Andrea said quietly. 'But you are directing your arguments at quite the wrong person, I'm afraid. It is Blaise you need to convince, and he is determined, I know, to keep Philippe here with him, no matter what the cost.'

Simone pitched her cigarette to the floor, and ground it savagely under her heel.

'The cost already has been quite—considerable—has it not?' She laughed softly. '*Le pauvre* Blaise. Almost I can pity him. It cannot suit his pride to be saddled with a wife he does not want merely for the sake of a child. I was not deceived, you understand, by this hasty wedding. An affair in a corner, was it not?'

'Hole-and-corner is the phrase you are searching for, I think,' Andrea said wearily. 'But you're wrong, *mademoiselle*. It may have begun like that, I'm willing to admit, but

I—I love Blaise and I hope and believe that he is beginning to love me,' she ended, her heart throbbing painfully, as she dared to voice for the first time the truth of her feelings and desires.

Simone's small teeth glinted. 'Your sentiments are charming, *madame*—naïve and sentimental, but charming. I have no doubt that Blaise will be happy to oblige you. He was not meant to lead a celibate life,' she went on, a frankly reminiscent smile curving her lips. 'You will have nothing to complain of in his expertise as a lover, if you can once overcome your revulsion at his face. I could not—even now,' she added with a little shrug.

The bright blaze of confidence in Andrea died as swiftly as it had sprung to life. She stared unbelievingly at Simone, her brain refusing to credit the obvious implications of the other girl's words.

'What do you mean?' It might have been someone else's voice.

Simone looked pityingly at her. 'It is true, *n'est-ce pas*? You really don't know that Blaise and I were once engaged to be married.'

'Before the fire at Belle Rivière?' Andrea said through stiff lips.

'*Naturellement*. Afterwards, when they brought him out and I saw what had happened to his face, I was a coward, I admit. I have not a strong stomach for such things. I knew I could never let him touch me again. It was painful for us both, but in the end easier for me than attempting to hide such feelings. That would have been impossible.'

There was almost a touch of complacency in her tone, Andrea thought wildly, as if she expected her to agree and sympathise.

Simone went on, 'Now you can comprehend why Blaise is so anxious to have custody of Philippe. It is his revenge on me for having broken our engagement.' She sighed elaborately. 'It is strange to think how easily I might have been Madame Levallier at this moment.' She stretched sensuously, and met Andrea's horrified gaze. 'He still wants me, you know,' she said almost idly. 'But I have made him see it is impossible. Even if it were not for the scars, you are his wife and deserve his loyalty if nothing else. You should be grateful to me.'

'Thank you.' Andrea's voice was level and totally colourless. 'And now, if you'll excuse me.'

'*Certainement.*' Simone moved to one side to allow her to pass. '*Un moment*,' she added suddenly as Andrea reached the stairs. 'I have given you Blaise, after all. Surely you owe me Philippe in return.'

Andrea turned to face her, gathering her last reserves of emotional strength.

'I owe you nothing, *mademoiselle*. As for Philippe, you don't deserve him—neither you nor Blaise.'

She held her head high as she mounted the stairs. But her self-possession was a veneer, and carried her only round the curve of the stairs out of the sight of the watcher in the hall below. Once there, all the strength seemed to drain from her legs and she sank down on the wide stair, a long convulsive sob of agony tearing its way out of her being.

Andrea never knew how she got through the rest of that interminable day. Somewhere, operating independently outside herself, there seemed to be a girl who prepared food she could not have forced herself to eat, who cleaned silver until it gleamed, and used wax polish on furniture until her arms and shoulders ached with the exertion.

She was a strange creature, this girl. She could smile and speak and listen to what was said to her, in spite of the pain that seemed to be splitting her apart. She was even quite attractive too, in spite of her pallor, she thought critically as she caught a glimpse of herself in a mirror she was cleaning. Not in Simone's class, of course, yet sufficiently appealing for it to be quite reasonable for a man who wanted Simone and could not have her to console himself with her.

She could not complain, the sensible hard-working side

of her told this hysterical stranger who kept getting in her way. Blaise had never hinted that their relationship would mean any more to him than a purely physical release. It was she who had spoken the word 'love' in that connotation, and she could only be thankful she had not said it to him. What would he have done? she found herself wondering. Would he have pitied her, and pretended? It was unthinkable—unbearable, and she bit her lip until the blood came.

At least now his terms had been spelled out to her, and it was for her to decide whether or not they were acceptable.

When Gaston entered the dining room to make up the fire, she heard herself asking him quite calmly and normally if he had seen Monsieur Philippe, and nodding almost brightly when she was informed that the little one was walking with Mademoiselle Delatour.

The whole world seemed to be full of the splash of water, as the melting snow dripped from the eaves and ledges, and then, as the afternoon lengthened into approaching darkness, it began to rain, a steady persistent downpour.

Strange to think how she would have welcomed this rapid thaw only twenty-four hours earlier. Now she found herself anticipating the imminence of Simone's departure with something like dread.

Over and over again, she wondered why Blaise had not told her that Simone had been the fiancée who had rejected him after he had been injured. She dragged off the betrothal ring he had given her and left it on the dressing table in their room, unable to bear the thought of it occupying Simone's finger before her own.

She had a bath before dinner in the hope that the warm water would relax her, but it failed miserably. She was as taut as a violin string as she sat at the dressing table brushing her hair, and waiting with thudding heart for the sound of Blaise's approaching feet down the corridor.

When at last he came, she laid the brush down on the dressing table with suddenly nerveless fingers. She looked as white as a ghost, yet she did not trust her hands to apply blusher and lipstick with their usual sophistication.

He paused just inside the door and their eyes met in the mirror. He smiled, and for one heart-stopping moment she wondered how she could ever have thought his face bleak and hard, and a silent cry of anguish welled up inside her.

He crossed the room with his long swift stride, and bent over her, pressing his lips to the curve of her neck under her ear. The caress sent a shiver of response through her which she was unable to dissemble, and she heard him draw a sharp breath, then seek her mouth with his with a burning intensity which threatened to overwhelm her.

'A black dress?' he murmured teasingly at last against her lips, his long fingers slipping questingly inside the deep cowl collar to explore the delicate hollows and curves of her throat and shoulders. 'What are you in mourning for, *ma belle*?'

She wanted to cry out, 'For the rest of our lives together,' but she crushed the words down, and made herself smile.

'I—I thought it was *très chic*. Don't you like it?'

'I'm not sure.' Pretending to frown, he surveyed her, his head slightly on one side, from the allure of the tight-fitting bodice clinging to the uptilted breasts to the bell of a skirt which swung from her slender waist. 'I suppose it has its—compensations.'

In a sudden panic she felt the long zip at the back of the dress give way under the pressure of his fingers.

'Don't tremble so, *ma mie*.' There was a lazy sensuousness in his voice which sent hectic colour flying to her face. 'As you dressed this evening, you must have known that ultimately I would want to—undress you.'

'But—not now—not like this.' Feverishly she twisted herself free. 'Blaise—please. Dinner will be served. Everyone will be waiting for us.'

'Let them wait.' Effortlessly he captured her again, his mouth parting hers with a sensual mastery that sent flickers of fire racing through her veins. Desperately she snatched at the dress he was easing from her shoulders, holding it against her.

'Blaise, no. We—we must go down. Let me go—please!'

For a long moment he was very still, then he raised his head slowly and looked at her, his eyes holding a chill glitter that almost unnerved her.

Then, 'If that is your wish, *madame*,' he said bitingly, and released her so suddenly that she swayed and almost fell. With insolent casualness he pulled her dress into place and closed the zip with one long savage tug. He made her a slight, formal bow. 'On your way, *ma femme*. Make my apologies and tell everyone that I shall join them presently.'

Andrea's legs were shaking violently as she left the bedroom and she stumbled and nearly fell on the stairs. She stopped dead and made herself take several long deep breaths, seeking to regain her composure.

Simone was the sole occupant of the dining room when she entered, standing by the window slim and wraith-like in a white dress with softly floating sleeves and skirt, and the merest hint of a bodice. She smiled as Andrea came in, a smile at once so knowing and malicious that it was as if she had been a silent witness to the scene which had just transpired.

Andrea's fists clenched in the folds of her skirt. She looked round the room.

'Where is Philippe?'

'He is having a tray in his room.' Simone walked to the sideboard and poured herself an aperitif. She raised her glass towards Andrea in a mock toast. '*Salut*. I think he may have caught a chill from all his exploits in the snow.'

'Oh.' Andrea paused, then half-turned to the door. 'I think I'll just go and see how he is.'

'As you wish.' Simone lifted an indifferent shoulder. 'But he is probably asleep by now, and you might wake him.'

'I can promise I won't,' Andrea flung back over her shoulder.

There was a nightlight burning on the table beside

Philippe's bed, and he was lying on his back one arm flung free of the covers. His forehead seemed slightly warm, but his breathing was normal. Andrea drew the cover gently up over his shoulder and stole away again down the narrow stair.

As she approached the dining room again, she heard the murmur of voices within and guessed that Blaise had come downstairs. She took another deep breath before opening the door, and paused abruptly on the threshold.

Simone was standing in front of Blaise at the fireplace, so close that their bodies were almost touching. He was holding a glass and as Andrea watched Simone's hand went up and closed round his. Involuntarily Andrea stepped forward and Blaise's head came round sharply. He stepped away from Simone and the look he sent her contained an unmistakable warning.

'Would you like a drink?' His voice was cool and courteous, containing neither hidden passion nor veiled anger. She accepted stiffly, tempted for a moment to apologise for her intrusion but realising just in time that it would be more dignified to pretend she had noticed nothing.

'You are very pale, *ma chère*.' Simone's voice was all silky concern. 'I hope you have not taken the same chill as Philippe.'

'I hardly think so. I—I have a slight headache, that's all.' It was not a total lie. There was a hard knot of tension lodged just above her eyes.

It was a difficult meal. Simone chattered gaily throughout, indulging in a flood of nostalgia and reminiscence to which Blaise made little response or contribution. She made a point, every now and then, of turning to Andrea and deliberately drawing her into the conversation, asking if she knew places and people, requesting her opinions, which only served to emphasise Andrea's own feeling of isolation. She knew what Simone was up to, of course. She was reviving old intimacies along with the memories, and showing Andrea to be the outsider, none too subtly at that.

She picked at her food, finding Blaise's eyes on her, hard and ironic as she laid down her fork.

'Has your appetite for dinner suddenly deserted you, *ma mie*?'

She shrank inwardly from the edge in his voice, knowing only too well what it implied. When Madame Bresson brought in coffee, she felt she could stand no more and rising to her feet excused herself in a few incoherent words and got out of the room.

If there had been a key in the elaborate lock of Blaise's bedroom door, then she would have used it, and braved his undoubted anger. With set lips, she found the blankets and made up the bed on the couch. If he would not sleep there, then she would. She hesitated for a long time over undressing, deciding eventually there was little to be gained by remaining in the clothes she had worn at dinner. That decision made, it seemed important to get into her nightgown and long cream silk dressing gown as swiftly as possible, and her fingers were trembling as she tightened the sash round her slim waist. Normally, she lowered all the bedroom lamps before retiring, but tonight she decided she would leave them all full on. She needed to avoid the intimacy of the darkened room.

She walked restlessly over to the window, and pulled the curtain aside. A chill draught played on her face and the air was full of the scent of rain. Shivering, she let the curtain fall back and folded her arms tightly across her breasts. She wandered round the room, making tiny adjustments to the furniture and drapes, fiddling with the jars and bottles on the dressing table. She was tired, but she knew that even if she lay down for a while, she would not be able to sleep. All those nights when she had pretended to sleep, and now it was denied her. It was like a joke turned sour.

She bent to smooth a non-existent crease in the bedcover and stopped. There had been no hint of his silent approach. He stood just inside the door, leaning back against the panels, his eyes appraising her. The silence dragged. Eventually he said:

'This morning I held a woman in my arms—a woman who I knew wanted me as completely as I wanted her. I've carried the memory and the promise of that woman with me all day. Where did she go, Andrée, and who is this frigid hostile child who has taken her place?'

Whatever she had expected from him, it wasn't this.

'That isn't fair,' she protested weakly.

'I am not concerned with your English notion of fair play.' His voice cut at her, then gentled. 'I require a simple answer to a very simple question. I am here, after all, to claim my woman. I want to make sure she exists.'

His eyes went past her to the couch with its waiting blankets and pillow and they narrowed.

'What does that mean?' The softness of his voice was deceptive, she knew.

'Don't make things difficult, Blaise,' she appealed. 'After all, nothing has really changed ...'

'Everything has changed, and you know it,' he interrupted without a change in inflection. 'The comedy is over, *ma mie*. You are my wife and I intend that you shall share my bed.'

She took a hasty step backwards, stumbling over the hem of her robe, and he grinned mockingly. He took off his coat and pitched it on to a chair. His tie followed it, and he began to unfasten his shirt. He sent her a sardonic look.

'Don't look so appalled, *chérie*. Why not get into bed and pretend to be asleep as you usually do? Just don't rely on the fact that I'll be too much of a gentleman to wake you.' He waited for a moment, then stripped off his shirt and tossed it on to the floor. 'No? Then come here.' He held out his arms to her. She did not move and he uttered an impatient sigh. 'Don't make me fetch you, Andrée.'

'I hate you,' she whispered out of the welter of confusion and misery that possessed her.

He gave a slight shrug. 'As you wish,' he said calmly. 'It will make no difference.' He walked over to her, and stood looking down into her face. His own was impassive, but there was an expression in his eyes that terrified her.

'How can a woman change so much in just a few short hours?' he said, half to himself. 'I should have obeyed my instincts, *ma belle*, and taken you this morning. But no matter.'

His hands reached out and gripped her shoulders, then slid the length of her body to the slight swell of her hips, drawing her inexorably forward into his arms. She tried to struggle, to pull away, but his arms were steel bands imprisoning her.

'This morning was different,' she said wildly.

'Yet we are the same people. So, this morning would have been for pleasure, and tonight, for some reason best known to yourself, it has to be for duty.' His kiss was lingering, a calculated insult. 'So be it, *chérie*. The decision is yours.'

He lifted her off her feet and strode with her to the bed. A sob of entreaty welled up in her throat but was stifled by his mouth on hers. She lay in his arms, shamed and helpless, every sense she possessed screaming a response to the cynical expertise with which his hands and lips were exploring her body.

'Name of God, Andrée,' he whispered at last, 'be a little merciful. Don't force me to take you like this.'

'You ask too much.' Her voice trembled. 'I'm only your wife, remember? I'm here out of duty, you said so yourself. If you want more, why don't you seek out Simone again? She seems only too willing to relent towards you.'

His face was diabolic for an instant, and she shrank instinctively, but he shook his head.

'No, *ma belle*, I shan't hit you. By morning you will have been punished enough, I think.'

Somewhere a long way off someone was screaming. For a dreadful moment she thought it was herself, and she was ashamed. Surely she could endure this—this loveless possession without uttering a sound. Did she want to give him the satisfaction of seeing her grovel?

Then she realised there was silence in the room, and that she was free. That the weight of his body no longer pinned hers to the bed. He was lying on his side, his head turned from her, listening intently. The screams came again, quavering and recognisable.

'Philippe!' she gasped, panic gripping her. Blaise was already on his feet, shrugging himself into a towelling dressing gown. He picked her robe up from the floor and tossed it to her. He had left the room before she had even huddled it round her.

The screams were ear-piercing as she flung herself into the tower. Madame Bresson was before them, bending over the bed, trying unavailingly to hush the child who was cowering at the end of his bed, his mouth an 'o' of pure terror. She turned as they entered.

'Oh, Monseigneur—Madame!'

'*Tais-toi*, Philippe. *Qu-as tu*?' Blaise strode to the bed and made to pick the child up. Philippe uttered another shriek and dived headlong on to the floor, landing at Andrea's feet. His arms went convulsively around her legs, and she almost overbalanced at the impact. His white tear-stained face stared imploringly up at her.

'La Cicatrice,' he wept. 'La Cicatrice has come for me. Oh, make him go away!'

'Hush, darling!' Andrea gently unclasped the clinging arms and knelt down beside him. 'I'm here. Nothing can hurt you. Have you been dreaming?' She smoothed the tousled hair back from his damp forehead.

'He was here,' Philippe insisted between hiccupping sobs. 'He came for me. There was nowhere for me to hide. He was going to kill me.'

'What nonsense is this?' Blaise walked forward restlessly, and Philippe let out another high-pitched wail.

'La Cicatrice!'

'My sweet, that is your Uncle Blaise who loves you and wants to take care of you.' Andrea spoke as soothingly as she knew how. 'Someone has been telling you a lot of silly stories, and you have got them jumbled in your poor head, that's all. And then you went to sleep and had a horrid dream. But it's gone now.'

Philippe buried his head in the silk of her robe. 'Make him go!' came his muffled entreaty.

Andrea looked up appealingly at Blaise. His face was icy with fury, a betraying muscle jerking in his cheek.

'Leave him with Clothilde,' he directed uncompromisingly, and reached down for her wrist. 'Come.'

'Leave Tante Andrée alone. You're a wicked man and she doesn't want to go with you.' Philippe's head jerked round and for a painful instant he buried small white teeth in his uncle's wrist.

'*Diable!*' Blaise snatched his hand away, grimly inspecting the row of bright red crescents in his flesh. Madame Bresson pressed her hand to her mouth in fascinated horror and Andrea waited dry-mouthed for the explosion of wrath to come.

But it did not come. Blaise's lips suddenly relaxed their grimness and a faint rueful smile appeared.

'You seem to have acquired a protector, *madame*. *Eh bien*, stay with him for a while, if you must, until he goes back to sleep, but don't keep me waiting too long. As for you, *monsieur mon neveu*, you and I will have a little talk in the morning, and you can tell me these—stories of yours. They interest me profoundly.'

As he disappeared down the stairs, Andrea felt Philippe draw a long ragged breath of relief.

'Let me take him, *madame*.' Madame Bresson, securely wrapped in a blue woollen garment, her hair in braids, bustled forward, her face full of concern. '*Pauvre petit*.'

Andrea shook her head. 'No, I'll stay with him for a while. You—you heard Monseigneur. As soon as he is asleep, I'll call you and perhaps you'll sit with him for a while in case he wakes again.'

They put Philippe back into bed and drew the covers over him. Andrea fetched a chair and placed it beside the bed. As she settled herself, Philippe's hand crept from under the bedding and took hers. Madame gave a sentimental sigh and departed.

'Now we are alone,' Philippe remarked with something like content.

'Yes,' Andrea said gently. 'Philippe, *chéri*, what frightened you so?'

'La Cicatrice came.' The child's eyes were wide and earnest in the flickering light. 'He was going to kill me, and throw my body down into the courtyard.'

'But you call your uncle Blaise La Cicatrice,' Andrea pointed out. 'And he could not possibly have come into your room because he was with me. Besides, darling, he doesn't want to hurt you. Your papa before he died said that your Uncle Blaise was to look after you because he knew that he would love you and be kind to you.'

Oh God, let it be the truth, she added silently, recalling all her early misgivings about the situation when she had first come to St Jean des Roches and wondered what kind of bleak outlook the chateau would hold for a child.

She felt Philippe wriggle slightly, but he seemed quite calm again, so she pressed on.

'Philippe, who told you that the other man—the man in history who killed Marie-Denise's boy—had a scar on his face?'

After a long silence. 'I don't remember,' Philippe said sullenly.

'I think you do. I think it was the same person who told you about the tower and everything that has happened here.'

Another silence. Then Philippe said almost beseechingly, 'It was a bedtime story. I—I like such stories. You must not be angry with Tante Simone.'

'I'm not angry.' Andrea fought to keep her voice calm. 'But sometimes even Tante Simone gets things wrong. You see, Marie-Denise's husband didn't have a scar on his face. He had never been brave and tried to save someone's life like Uncle Blaise. There's a portrait of him somewhere in the chateau, I expect. We'll have a look tomorrow. Then you'll see he has no scar.'

Philippe remained silent for a time, then he burst out,

'But Uncle Blaise does want to kill me—for the money, like he killed my papa.'

'Money?' Andrea was puzzled. This was the first mention of any money.

Philippe sat up. 'The money for Belle Rivière—after it was burned,' he said. 'My Uncle Blaise set fire to Belle Rivière to get the money.'

'You mean Belle Rivière was insured?'

Philippe nodded rather doubtfully. 'For many thousands of francs. My Uncle Blaise needed that money, so he set fire to the house and Papa died.'

Andrea felt cold and sick. Something was beating at the door of her memory. Something Blaise had said about Jean-Paul's death. She strained to remember it, to remember his actual words. Surely he had said—hadn't he—that he could have stopped it, that it need never have happened. Was it true, then? Had Blaise set fire to the plantation house for the insurance money and set in motion the chain of events which would lead to his brother's death? If so, then there was good reason for his guilt and bitterness.

'If I die too,' said Philippe, 'then the money will come to my Uncle Blaise. He is poor now, but with that money he would be rich.'

'Hush, darling.' Andrea's voice was steady. 'Try not to think about it any more. Lie down now, and go to sleep.'

She felt as if someone had struck her a violent blow in the face. She was quite numb, but very soon the pain would start.

Long after Philippe's breathing proclaimed the fact that he was asleep, she sat motionless beside his bed, her tired mind endlessly pursuing the treadmill of fact and interference. There was a dreadful, inevitable logic behind the whole thing. It explained so much, particularly his obsession with gaining custody over Philippe. It was obvious that he would not want Simone to have the boy. He had once been her fiancé, and her lover, and she would know, better than anyone, the forces that drove him. Had there been an oblique warning intended when she had told Andrea that Philippe would be better off with her? And was it just the damage to his face that had turned her against him, or was there a deeper, more sinister reason?

She gave a little sob and buried her face in her hands. And this was the man with whom she had fallen hopelessly and irrevocably in love. Only Philippe's nightmare had prevented him from gaining possession of her, body as well as soul. Now she too was part of that nightmare.

Feverish thoughts chased through her brain. By the following day the roads would be passable again. She could leave. But if she went, what would happen to Philippe? No matter what the cost to herself in emotional terms, she had to stay for his sake, or else take him with her.

For an agonising moment Blaise's face seemed to swim in front of her, his eyes caressing her, desiring her. She could almost fool herself into thinking—loving her.

She pressed her hand convulsively against her quivering lips. She would not go to him now. She could not. Once again in his arms, under the spell of his lovemaking, she knew right and wrong would lose all meaning for her.

Tomorrow she would face him. She would have more strength then to confront him with her knowledge. What would happen after that, she thought bleakly, she could not even conjecture.

She leaned back in the chair, gazing sightlessly at the wall.

'Oh, Blaise,' she whispered agonisedly. 'Whatever you've done—whatever you are—God help me, but I love you.'

CHAPTER NINE

It was past dawn when Andrea let herself out of the tower and back into the main part of the building. She had slept only fitfully and her limbs were cramped and aching.

She walked slowly along the corridor to the bedroom,

dreading the inevitable confrontation. Apart from anything else, Blaise would be angry that she had not relinquished Philippe into Madame Bresson's care and come back to him. In some ways, cowardly though it was, she wished she had done just that. At this very moment she could have woken in his arms, sated and fulfilled, happy in her ignorance.

It took all the courage she possessed to push open the bedroom door and walk in. And he was not there.

Andrea glanced round, puzzled. The bed, though slightly rumpled, had clearly not been slept in, and the couch bore no signs of occupation either. Yet he had been there, because all the lamps were not extinguished, and the only illumination was provided by the pale early morning light filtering through the curtains.

She sank down on the edge of the bed and buried her face in her hands, overcome by her own weariness. She supposed she should dress and seek Blaise out to tell him what she had learned, but surely there would be no harm if she lay down, just for a few minutes, and rested her head on the pillow. Her eyelids felt as if lead weights had been attached to them. She would close them for a minute. Only for a minute, she promised herself drowsily. Nothing could happen while she just closed her eyes for a minute.

But as soon as she closed them, someone was shaking her arm gently but persistently, forcing her to wake up again. She struggled up through thick layers of sleep to find Madame Bresson standing at her bedside with a tray of coffee.

'This is very early,' she struggled on to one elbow.

Madame looked at her in mild astonishment. '*Qu-avez-vous, madame*? It is past ten hours.'

'It can't be!' Andrea stared at her wristwatch in consternation, but the evidence simply confirmed what Madame Bresson had just said. She had slept for over five hours.

Madame reached into her apron pocket. 'And this has come for you, *madame*.' She produced a letter with an

English stamp. 'The first mail for a week has got through, praise to *le bon dieu*.'

She smiled maternally at Andrea and left her to the enjoyment of her coffee and her letter. It was Aunt Marion's handwriting, and Andrea knew a qualm as she tore open the envelope. She had written a brief and somewhat laconic account of her sudden marriage to her family, and hoped that Clare would have learned enough sense to keep her mouth shut and not make a bad situation worse by belated and unwanted confessions of her part in the whole mess.

The fact that the letter began 'My dearest girl' was somehow reassuring, and as Andrea scanned through the lines, she breathed a sigh of relief. Clare seemed to be learning an element of discretion at long last.

Aunt Marion and Uncle Max were naturally shocked to hear of her marriage and disappointed she should have chosen to marry in such an apparently hurried and secretive manner, her aunt wrote. But if she was happy, that was all that mattered, and they were looking forward with great interest to meeting Andrea's husband when she brought him to London—and the little boy, of course.

'We think it is very brave of you, darling, to take on a ready-made family,' wrote Aunt Marion. 'Marriage always needs a great deal of adjustment in the early stages, and this is easier if only the two of you are involved. Why not let Philippe come to us for a few weeks so that you and Blaise can make the most of your honeymoon? Your uncle says you've chosen to live in a most exciting part of France, although I understand it can be rather wild and stormy.'

The letter concluded with all sorts of affectionate messages for them both, and the urgent hope that they would be able to get to England for Clare's wedding, now less than a month away.

Andrea looked down at the letter with tear-blurred eyes. They were such darlings, and they had accepted without question her rather evasive story about having met Blaise in London through her P.R. work.

And they had given her the loophole she needed. All

she had to do now was persuade Blaise to allow her to take Philippe to London to Clare's wedding with her. What she would do once they were safely there, she had no idea, but Uncle Max would know whom to consult over the legalities of the situation.

She put down the letter and began to sip her coffee. The brief sleep had cleared her head to some extent, and somehow she would have to find the courage to get through the day.

She washed quickly, splashing her face with cold water to banish any lingering drowsiness, and dressed in the jeans and dark sweater that she normally wore during the daytime.

As she emerged into the corridor, one thought had crystallised above all others. For her own peace of mind as well as Philippe's, she would move him out of the tower. She would clear out one of the big gloomy rooms along this corridor, and have his small bed moved into it—and she would sleep there with him.

Her steps faltered slightly as pain lashed at her again. Twenty-four hours ago, she thought, remembering those sensuous moments in Blaise's arms. Not so very long a time in which to have been shown the possibility of paradise, and then had it snatched away.

Acting on blind impulse, she seized the ornate handle of the door she was passing, twisted it and went into the darkened room. She dragged back the dusty curtains and stood back to take a critical appraisal. Yes, there were possibilities, she supposed, massive and overpowering though the room was, with its dark tapestry panels on the walls and solid furniture. She would start turning it out at once, and with any luck she and Philippe would be able to move in that night.

With a nod of determination she moved to the door, and paused. Someone was coming along the passage with a swift stride she knew only too well. The last thing she wanted on earth at that moment was to meet Blaise face to face, and she slipped back behind the heavy door, praying that he would not notice it was slightly ajar and decide to investigate. At the same time, she knew it was more than she could bear not to catch so much as a glimpse of him, and with a slight harsh intake of breath she peeped out through the crack in the door.

Perhaps, because she was expecting him to be angry and bitter when she saw him next, the shock was all the greater. Swinging along the corridor, his hands thrust deep into his pants pockets, Blaise was smiling to himself. And not the sardonic quirk of the lips that could hurt her so much either. He was transformed again into the man she had glimpsed yesterday morning when he had made passionate love to her. The man who has suddenly found that the world is a good place to live in and whose cares and anxieties have sunk to infinitesimal proportions. As Andrea watched almost incredulously, he threw back his head suddenly and laughed, a relaxed, full-throated laugh that spoke predominantly of pure satisfaction. Almost directly opposite where Andrea was concealed, he turned for an instant and stared back along the way he had come. Then he laughed again, and walked on.

The sound of his step had died away completely when Andrea finally emerged. Totally perplexed, she stood for a moment staring down the corridor, trying to decide what had so amused him and brought about this incredible change in him. After all, there was nothing down that corridor except more vast bedrooms, all empty, except for the one that she had used and which Simone now occupied . . .

She stood very still while the words reverberated and re-echoed inside her skull. He had obviously not spent the night in his own room, therefore it followed that he must have slept elsewhere. The picture was imprinted on her memory. Blaise and Simone standing in intimate closeness in the dining room last night when she had blundered in. Simone's hand going up to caress his—and her own stupidly provocative remark suggesting that Simone's attitude towards him had changed and that he should seek her out.

Could she really complain if he had in fact done so?

Her hand stole up to her mouth like a frightened child's, and she wanted very badly to cry. To fling herself down on the worn carpet and scream and drum her heels in a rage of jealousy and fury.

Was it really possible, when he realised she was not going to return that night, that he had cynically gone to the bed of another woman? Andrea shook her head in desperate negation, trying to push away the images that followed in the train of such a thought. Was the happiness that had been so much in evidence just then the remembered joy of the lover? She caught her lip savagely in her teeth. If it was so, then whom could she blame but herself? Even before she had heard Philippe's story, she had allowed the thought of Blaise's past love for Simone to poison their relationship. She had found the thought of them together totally unbearable. Could this be because she knew he had never truly exorcised Simone from his mind and heart? That however generously she gave herself to him, her gift could only be second-best because he could not forget Simone and her rejection of him?

There were swift, scalding tears on her face, and she wiped them away with an unsteady hand. She must conserve all her emotional energy now. She was going to need it. All the resources she had left had to be devoted to one thing—finding the earliest opportunity for Philippe and herself to leave St Jean des Roches for ever.

She was calm but composed as she came downstairs two hours later. The bed in the big room upstairs had been stripped and was being aired, and the room itself had been swept and dusted and looked an altogether more cheerful sight. She carried the long curtains over her arm. The rain had stopped now, so she thought she would hang them over one of the washing lines and beat some of the dust out of them.

Gaston was coming through the hall as she reached the bottom of the stairs, and she called to him.

'Gaston. I have a job for you.'

'All in good time, *madame*. All in good time.' He sounded a little peevish. 'First, I must bring down the baggage of Mademoiselle Delatour and put it in her car.'

'Baggage?' Andrea's heart gave an uneven beat. 'Do you mean—is Mademoiselle Delatour leaving?'

Gaston shrugged. 'The road to the village is open again, *madame*. Why should she stay?'

He went past her up the stairs, grumbling under his breath. Andrea stood stock still, clutching the dusty curtains against her. Simone leaving, she thought wildly. It couldn't be true—not now, when she had every reason, it would seem, to stay. Or did Blaise jib at the fact of keeping his mistress under the same roof as his wife and was merely sending her to be a discreet distance away? She made her way slowly to the kitchen area, her mind whirling with conjecture.

Madame Bresson greeted her with a broad smile and an offer of hot coffee, which she accepted.

'So Mademoiselle Delatour leaves us today, *madame*?' the housekeeper remarked, pouring the rich dark liquid into the beakers. 'It is a good thing for *le petit*, I think, that she does so.'

'Oh?' Andrea digested this. 'Why do you say that?'

Madame's lip curled. 'I am not blind, *madame*. Can I not see what she is about, that one? Each night I take *le petit* warm milk when he is in bed and each night it is the same. He is terrified of every shadow that moves because of Mademoiselle his aunt and her—bedtime stories!' She gave Andrea a shrewd glance which seemed to encompass her pale cheeks and the deep shadows beneath her eyes. 'She has not the gift of kindness, as you have, *madame*. All will go well when she departs, you will see.'

Andrea gave a strained smile. 'I wish I could believe that,' she said in a low voice. She had to resist the temptation to put her head on Madame's motherly bosom and sob out all her fears and apprehensions, purging herself of jealousy and anger at the same time. But it would not be fair, she knew. Madame had served the Levallier family all her life, and it would be wrong to burden her with this and divide her loyalties in such a way.

The door opened and Gaston marched in, mopping his brow.

'Monseigneur is seeking you, *madame*,' he told Andrea in a surly tone.

Andrea swallowed. The moment she had dreaded had come at last. The only wonder was that she had been spared for so long.

She stood up. 'Gaston, will you go to Monsieur Philippe's room in the tower and dismantle his bed again. I—we're moving him into the house for a night or two. I'll show you which room we—he will be using.'

Gaston cast his eyes to heaven. '*Sacre bleu*, madame! Have you forgotten? To take that bed into the tower—*quelle affaire*! And now it must descend again—and after the baggage of Mademoiselle!'

Andrea gave him a sweet smile. 'I think you'll survive,' she said callously.

As she went into the hall, she saw that the great door was standing open and that Simone's car was drawn up outside in the courtyard. Even as she registered this, Simone herself appeared. She looked slightly less immaculate than usual. Her hair was dishevelled and she seemed rather out of breath.

'Have you come to see me safely off the premises, Andrée?' she inquired silkily.

'I hardly think that's necessary.' Andrea walked forward, forcing herself to speak calmly. She owed it to her pride, she thought, not to give Simone the slightest hint that she either knew or cared about last night.

'No.' Simone gave a slow nod. 'It has been—interesting, but I shall be glad to go now. I have achieved what I wished to do, though not in the way that I expected.' She smiled widely at Andrea, her eyes very bright. 'I leave you the pieces, *ma chère*. Put them together, if you can.'

For a moment Andrea seemed to her Philippe screaming again, to see his small face contorted with terrified sobs.

She took another step forward.

'I may not have the physical strength to throw you through that door, Simone,' she said levelly, 'but I'm more than willing to try.'

It gave her an incredible satisfaction to see how Simone backed hastily away. She half ran out to her car, fumbling her keys into the lock. The last look she sent over her shoulder to Andrea was full of open malice.

'Save your energies, *chérie*,' she called. 'You will need them all. Losers always do.'

The car door banged and the engine sprang into vibrating life. A minute later and there was only the faint haze from the exhaust to prove that she had ever been there. Andrea closed the massive door and leaned against it, conscious of a flood of relief.

Then very slowly she went to look for Blaise. He did not appear to be anywhere downstairs and it took all the courage she possessed to mount the stairs again and go to the room she had shared with him for those few brief nights.

He was standing at the window staring out. Watching Simone depart? Wondering when he would be—with her again? Andrea let her thoughts run mad, tormenting her as she closed the door and waited for him to turn round and register the fact that she was there.

Without moving he said quietly, 'I waited for you for a long time last night, Andrée.'

She moistened her lips. 'Philippe needed me,' she said flatly.

'And my need for you? That counted for nothing, I suppose.'

'I—I couldn't leave Philippe,' she said defensively after a pause. 'Anyway, you had—consolation.' She could have bitten her tongue out as soon as the words were uttered.

He turned then and looked at her, and the amazing thing was he still didn't seem to be angry. He was even smiling faintly.

'The whisky bottle? Yes—once I would have turned to that, but no longer. Now when I am wounded, Andrée, I shall come to you to be healed.'

She stared at the floor. 'I can't even heal myself.'

'Then we must heal each other.' He walked across the room to her and stood, studying her averted face. His hand went out to lift her chin. 'Look at me, *ma belle.*'

She twisted wildly away out of the reach of his hands. 'Don't touch me!'

He gave a soft laugh. 'Oh, but I shall, *mon amour*. Whenever and however I wish, until you stop fighting me in that stubborn little head of yours and learn to be a woman.'

'I've already learned all I need to know.' She stared up at him. 'You—you're an expert teacher, Blaise, but school's out now.' She swallowed. 'You remember my cousin Clare. Well, she's getting married soon and I would like to go to her wedding.'

'How could I ever forget your cousin Clare?' the old sardonic note was back in his voice, but there was amusement as well. 'No doubt we can arrange something, although it will not be easy for me to get away.'

Andrea shook her head. 'There's no need for you to get away,' she said breathlessly. 'I would like to go on my own, please, or perhaps take Philippe with me. My aunt has invited us to have a short holiday with them.'

There was a long silence. When she ventured another glance at him, she saw he was looking down at her with narrowed eyes.

'Why am I not to come with you?'

'Well,' she improvised desperately, 'for one thing, it would be very awkward for Clare and ...'

'The truth, Andrée.' His voice was still quiet, but it held a trace of steel.

'I think it would be a good idea if I went away for a while and took Philippe with me,' she said, avoiding his gaze. 'I think Philippe needs to get away. He—he isn't happy here.'

'Nevertheless this is his home—the only one he possesses now.'

'Yes,' she said. 'As you have cause to remember.'

Blaise took her by the shoulders, his fingers bruising her skin.

'And what, my sweet wife, do you mean by that?' he asked softly.

She shook her head, tears welling up uncontrollably in her eyes.

'Answer me, damn you!' His fingers gripped tighter, forcing a cry from her lips.

'Blaise, let us go. Take the money, and Philippe and I will never bother you again. I—I can support him. I might even be able to get my old job back in London . . .' The expression on his face brought her to a stumbling silence.

'What money?' he said too evenly.

'The insurance money—for Belle Rivière.' She was beginning to feel faint under the stress of the moment, and the harsh, gruelling pressure of his hands. 'Philippe knows all about it, Blaise. That's why he has been so frightened. He—he can't be sure that his father's death was an accident. He thinks he might be next. If I can get him away, then he may forget all about it in time and learn to be a child again.'

His face was white under his tan, the scar standing out in angry prominence along his cheek. There was anger in his eyes, too, and contempt, and a kind of hopelessness that cut her to the heart.

'If anyone else had said that to me,' he said at last, his voice hoarse, almost unrecognisable, 'I think I would have killed them.' He wrenched his hands away from her as if the touch of her skin was suddenly repugnant to him. She swayed and nearly fell.

'You were not the only one who received a letter today, *madame*.' He thrust his hand into the pocket of the coat he was wearing and produced a bulging envelope. 'If your command of my language does not enable you to translate, I will be happy to give you the gist of what it says. Take it.'

Shakily, she obeyed. There was a mass of documentation inside—official-looking forms and photostats, and at the front, a long letter with an indecipherable signature at the bottom.

She forced herself to read it, picking up key phrases which she could distinguish.

'Shall I assist you?' Blaise's finger stabbed at the papers. 'It comes, as you see, from an insurance company—the company which insured Belle Rivière. It tells me that they have now completed their investigations, and are satisfied that the fire at the house was deliberate arson. Therefore no payment will be made of any kind. As I think I once told you, *madame*, there is nothing left from Belle Rivière except the rent from the land. That is all Philippe possesses in the world—except my roof over his head and your unbounded sympathy,' he added savagely.

She stared at him, unable to take in what he was saying in its entirety.

'It was—arson?' she got out. 'And they know.'

His lip curled. 'Of course they know. They are not fools, these insurance companies. If Jean-Paul had been in his right mind, he would have known that. As it was, he staked everything he had on this one last desperate gamble, and he lost—everything. Including his own life.'

'Jean-Paul? Philippe's father set fire to Belle Rivière?' Horrific and tragic though the truth was, Andrea felt her heart lift within her in one wild leap of hope.

Blaise turned away abruptly, dragging his fingers wearily through his hair.

'Yes,' he said. 'And my one concern in this has been to make sure that Philippe never knew what really happened. I thought—I hoped that he would believe the fire had been an accident. I told myself his fear and loathing of me had been deliberately instigated by Simone—out of revenge.'

'I think it was,' Andrea said in a low voice, and shrank as she saw his face twist. 'Oh, Blaise, I'm sorry. I know you still love her, but . . .'

'What did you say?' he turned on her.

'I know you love Simone,' she said helplessly. 'And I know you spent the night with her.'

'*Dieu*,' he said softly. 'I am to be spared nothing, it seems. No slander is too great to be applied to my name. You think that because I was denied your body, I went to her.' He threw back his head and gave a short, savage laugh. 'Oh, no, *mon coeur*. When one has been granted a glimpse of heaven, one does not run straight to hell. When I realised that you were not coming back, I went out and walked—a long way over the hills. I left all my demons there—or thought I had. Today, I decided, we would start again, you and I, and when that letter came, it seemed like a sign. At last I could put all that business behind me. The truth was known, and one day when Philippe was old enough, I might be able to tell him about it.'

He put his hand quite gently under her chin, raising her face and studying it with an air of detached interest as if he had never seen her before.

'Did you never ask yourself, *ma mie*, why Simone should have departed in such haste this morning? I can tell you. Because I showed her this letter, and she knew she had nothing to gain any more. Why do you think she wanted Philippe? Because she loved him? Simone has never loved anyone or anything but herself. Apart from money, that is. She has a charming body, and she knows well how to barter it to get what she desires. For a time she desired me, but I was not rich, so she decided to make arrangements. Who do you suppose suggested to Jean-Paul that one way out of his difficulties would be to burn down Belle Rivière?' He smiled sardonically at Andrea's gasp. 'It is true, I assure you. You thought that she discarded me solely because of this.' He touched his scarred face. 'It was only partly true. Simone threw me aside when she realised I was not prepared to play her dirty game and try and cover up what Jean-Paul had done. She did her best to persuade me—as she had done with him. Then she took Philippe. She still hoped that through him the money would be forthcoming.' Grimly he held up the letter. 'Now she knows differently.'

He pushed the papers back into his pocket, and looked

at her. His face looked tired and haggard and he made no attempt to touch her again.

'I thought,' he said quietly, 'that when you closed your eyes and turned away from me in revulsion on our wedding night nothing could ever hurt me again as much as that. I, too, know differently now. Go to London, Andrée. Take up your own life—I won't stop you. But Philippe stays here. It will not be easy, but at least I know now what I have to fight against.'

'Blaise.' Timidly she put out her hand, and, with a sense of shock, saw him recoil almost violently.

'I don't want your pity, Andrée. Your love I had hoped for—one day maybe—if I was patient and did not force you or frighten you.'

'I'm not frightened,' she whispered. 'Oh, Blaise, don't you know what I'm trying to say? I've done you a terrible wrong, I know, but ...'

He lifted a hand, silencing her. 'Don't let us talk of wrongs, *ma belle*. I wronged you when I made you marry me. But it is not too late to make amends. I won't hold you to your promise of a year. It might be better if you went quite soon.'

She gave a little shuddering sigh, conscious that somewhere close at hand, someone was running with heavy blundering footsteps.

'Blaise ...' she began, and then the door behind them burst open and Gaston came in.

'Monseigneur,' he gasped out. '*Le petit* Philippe. He is nowhere to be found. We have been searching, all of us—Monsieur Alan too. His clothes are there, but he is gone.'

Blaise swore violently under his breath as he started forward.

'Did he go with Mademoiselle Delatour?' he demanded.

Gaston shrugged helplessly. 'I put the baggage in her car, Monseigneur. But no one saw her depart.'

'I saw her,' Andrea said. 'I didn't see Philippe, but she could have hidden him in the car. She seemed—strange.'

Blaise turned to Gaston. 'Get the Landrover out,' he

ordered. 'We'll go after her. She won't have got far—the roads are still bad in places.'

'May I go with you?' Andrea begged.

'No.' He did not look at her. 'Last night she mentioned that he was not well. You had best stay here and have a warm bed waiting for him. Ask your English friend to go to the village for the doctor.'

He went past her and out of the room followed by Gaston. Andrea followed more slowly, her mind dazed. Simone had taken Philippe—but for what reason? Pure malice was the only one that suggested itself. Her heart skipped a beat. Surely that was all it could be? Even Simone could not bring herself to actually harm the child. She had lied and schemed and done untold damage, but that was as far as she could go. Taking Philippe away with her could be no more than a defiant gesture.

It had been Madame Bresson who had discovered Philippe's disappearance, she learned. Madame had gone to waken him at the usual time, but he was sleeping so sweetly that she decided to leave him where he was. When she had returned, he had gone—apparently in his pyjamas, because all his day clothes were still neatly folded on the chair and nothing was missing from his wardrobe.

'*Le pauvre petit.*' Madame almost wrung her hands. 'How cold he will be! What could Mademoiselle have been thinking of?'

At first, Madame said, she had thought he might be hiding, or have run over to the gatehouse to see Alan. She and Gaston had combed the outbuildings and grounds calling to him when their search of the house had proved fruitless.

Andrea comforted the woman as best she could, pointing out that Simone was sure to have a car rug, and that Philippe was probably as warm at that moment as he had been in his own bed.

The following half hour seemed endless. She kept imagining that she heard the Landrover pulling back into the courtyard and dashing to the window, but everything was quiet—as quiet as the grave, she thought, and shivered.

There was little point in sitting about worrying, she decided, getting up restlessly. It would be more useful to start transferring Philippe's clothes and toys out of the tower to his new room. Positive thinking, she told herself ruefully.

In a way she was almost grateful to the crisis over Philippe. It stopped her from thinking about other things—about the look on Blaise's face when she had accused him of setting fire to Belle Rivière—the note in his voice when he had told her she was free to go. The way he had stepped back, as if he could no longer bear her to touch him. She swallowed convulsively. She must not think of these things now. When Philippe was safely back with them, then, perhaps, she would look at the ruin she had made of her marriage and see what could be salvaged. Simone had said she would leave her to pick up the pieces.

As she went up the stone stairs into Philippe's bedroom, her heart contracted at the sight of the still tumbled bed, and the litter of toys and books on the rug. He had not been allowed or given time to take anything with him, she thought.

Oh God, let them find him soon, she found herself praying. Let him be with Simone as long as he is safe. Don't let him just have run away. How long would a child without proper food or warm clothing last alone in that dank grey and white landscape? she wondered.

She walked over to the bed and began to smooth the quilt rather aimlessly. For the first time, the tower felt oppressive and sinister, its curved walls seeming to crowd around her. It had been the perfect atmosphere for Simone to spread her web, she thought. She had played right into her hands by choosing those particular rooms for Philippe. And of course Simone would have known the story of Marie-Denise. No one would be connected with the Levallier family for very long without getting to know the legend, she thought.

She sighed and turned back towards the door, and

paused abruptly, the hair lifting itself on the nape of her neck. She could hear a child crying.

Mentally she shook herself, telling herself that her imagination was playing tricks again. But the desolate wailing went on, quietly and hopelessly and very close at hand.

She swung round, staring round the small room, her heart beating fast and unevenly. 'Philippe?' she said sharply. She fell on her knees and looked under the bed. Nothing. She ran to the wardrobe, dragging open the doors and pulling the rack of clothes aside, but there was no small figure to be seen. And there was nowhere—nowhere else for a child to hide.

The wailing seemed to rise to a crescendo and then died away with a little whimper. It sounded as if it had come from over her head. But there was nothing up there—only pigeons and rafters and crumbling masonry, and besides, Gaston had secured the trapdoor, fastening it shut with big screws. She had seen him do it. She climbed up the steps and looked at the trapdoor overhead. It was still firmly shut, and the screws were still very much in place.

She shook her head bewilderedly and was preparing to descend again when she heard quite unmistakably a swift shuffling sound from the upper room. Pigeons, she thought, or—a rat. She put up a hand and pushed at the trap door, but it did not budge. She ran her fingers across one of the screws and winced as a splinter of wood became embedded in her flesh. She sucked it out and stared reflectively at Gaston's handiwork. It was odd, she thought, how rough the timber seemed round the screws. Yet he was usually so neat. I could have done as good a job as that, she thought critically, given the proper tools—a screwdriver and ... Her thoughts stopped. She was back in the stables again watching Gaston finishing off Philippe's sledge, and Simone was there too, perched on the edge of the table, playing with a screwdriver. She remembered at the time thinking how incongruous it had looked. And Gaston had missed some tools, she told herself. Tools which Philippe had been accused of borrowing and losing, but which he had denied.

She pressed her fingers against her forehead, forcing herself to think clearly.

Philippe's manner had been odd, she remembered. Could it have been that he knew that Simone had the tools, but did not wish to incriminate her? And the destruction of his sledge. It had been the obvious thing to assume it was Philippe's work, but could a small boy of his slight build really have wielded that kind of hammer with such devastating effect?

She reached up and rapped her knuckles on the trapdoor.

'Philippe!' she called again. She thought she heard a faint cry in answer, and that was enough. She turned, flinging herself down the narrow steps, out of the bedroom, and then down again. She flew to the door, cannoning into Alan who was just entering.

'Take it easy!' He took her by the shoulders and steadied her gently. 'The doctor's on his way and ...'

'He's up there,' she gulped. 'In the top room. She's put him up there and fastened the trapdoor. I've got to get some tools. I've got to get him out!'

Alan said sharply, 'You're joking. No one could do a thing like that to a sensitive kid.'

'She could.' Andrea tried to wrench free. 'She's capable of anything—I know that now. Alan, let me go. I've got to get him out.'

'You wait here. I'll go and see if there's a crowbar or something.'

'A screwdriver,' she said. 'That's what you need. There's a big one. She had it—I saw her, but I didn't realise.'

'Of course you didn't,' he said soothingly. 'Go back up there. Talk to him. Tell him help is coming. He trusts you.'

She went back up the stone stairs, wedging herself under the trapdoor, her mouth almost against the timbers. She called to Philippe, she sang, she told him funny stories, and all that came back to her was the echo of her own voice.

'Any luck?' Alan was there. 'No screwdriver anywhere. If she had it, she must have taken it with her. But there's this.' He held up a small but serviceable axe.

'He doesn't answer.' She stared at the axe. 'Alan, suppose he's there, over the trapdoor, when you break through.'

'Talk to him,' he said decisively. 'Tell him to get away as far as possible, and that we'll soon have him out of there.'

Numbly, she obeyed, then scrambled down out of the way as Alan prepared to take a swing at the trapdoor. The wood was old, and began to splinter after only a few blows.

'I'll cut a hole,' Alan gasped between strokes. 'Think you can—climb through?'

'I'll manage,' she said.

'It won't be very comfortable,' he warned. 'I ought to go ...'

'No,' she said, 'I'll do it. The hole doesn't need to be so big for me.'

The splintered wood dragged at her, catching in her sweater and tearing her jeans. Both her hands were bleeding as she scrambled through the trapdoor and knelt on the floor beyond it. Philippe was lying at one side of the room, huddled into a ball. He was unconscious and icily cold to the touch, but he was still breathing. Without a second's thought, Andrea tore off her sweater and wrapped him in it.

'Alan!' she screamed. 'He's here. Go and tell Clothilde. Blankets—lots of them and a drink—with brandy in it. A warm bath, even. And see if the doctor's here. I'll stay with him. Hurry!'

She heard Alan call an acknowledgment and the sound of his receding footsteps. She picked Philippe up in her arms and settled him across her lap, chafing his hands and bare feet. They were as cold as stones. She hugged him tightly, trying to imbue him with some of her own warmth. He gave a little shudder and opened his eyes. For a moment, she thought he did not know who she was.

'Philippe.' She bent and pressed her lips to his tangled hair. 'It's Tante Andrée.'

'Yes.' His eyelids flickered a little and a small, puzzled frown appeared. 'Is the game over?'

'Game?'

'I had to hide,' he said simply. 'Tante Simone was Marie-Denise and she said she would hide me from La Cicatrice so that he would never find me. But then she went, and it was cold and I was frightened.'

'Yes,' she said, her throat tight. 'The game is over. And soon you can have a nice sleep and a big bowl of soup.'

'*Bon.*' He gave her a long look. 'Tante Andrée, why are you not dressed?'

'Because you are wearing my sweater. You look very silly in it. The sleeves are too long and if I pull up the collar it looks as if there is no Philippe at all.'

He chuckled softly. 'That is silly,' he agreed. 'Because I am here.'

'Of course you are.'

'Tante Andrée, I don't want to play the game about Marie-Denise ever again. She broke my sledge, you know.'

'Marie Denise or Tante Simone?'

'I don't know.' His eyelids drooped again. 'I used to get muddled sometimes. Tante Simone said she *was* Marie-Denise, but I don't see how she could be.'

'No,' she said gently. 'No more than Uncle Blaise could have been La Cicatrice.'

He did not reply, and she did not say any more. It was a beginning, she thought.

She heard footsteps and voices in the room below and relaxed.

'Alan,' she called. 'Come up the stairs as far as you can and I'll pass him through to you.'

She carried Philippe awkwardly across the room, and knelt down by the hole.

'Look, *mon brave*,' she said. 'The silly door has stuck and I have to lower you through this hole. You can pretend that you are a parcel and I am posting you.'

He giggled feebly and she had to resist an impulse to hug him again.

'*Allons*. We must be careful, for there are lots of splinters. Keep still, *mon gars*. Parcels don't wriggle, you know.

That's right. And Alan will catch you.'

'No,' Blaise said. 'I will catch him.'

For one dreadful moment Andrea felt Philippe go tense and rigid in her arms. Then with a deep sigh, the stiffness seemed to go out of him. Blaise's hand gripped his legs securely and guided him down.

'Off with you, *petit*,' Andrea heard him say. 'Tante Andrée and I will come later to see how you are. The doctor is waiting to look at you.'

She heard Philippe mutter something sleepily in reply, and uttered a little prayer of thankfulness, conscious for the first time of how cold she herself was becoming. She peeped down through the hole in time to see Philippe being carried away by Gaston.

Blaise was speaking again. 'Do you wish to wait while we open the door properly?'

'No,' she said, her teeth beginning to chatter in spite of herself. 'I'm too cold. I think I'd rather brave the splinters again.'

She put her feet and legs gingerly into space, and felt them gripped and guided on to the top step. She slid through, scraping her arm and wincing a little. Blaise helped her down the steps in silence. Alan was standing at the bottom, still holding the axe.

'Well done,' he said awkwardly, and blushed.

She suddenly had a fair idea of the picture she must present—torn, dusty jeans and a brief lace bra which was no covering at all. As if he could read her thoughts, Blaise shrugged off his jacket and hung it round her shoulders. She thanked him and there was a long silence.

Alan cleared his throat. 'I'd better be going,' he said in a voice that sounded as if it was trying hard to be jocular and normal. He held up the axe. 'Better put this back.' He gave them an uncertain grin and went off whistling.

Andrea said in a subdued voice, 'He was very kind.'

'He is a little bit in love with you, I think,' Blaise said calmly.

'Oh.' She swallowed nervously. 'Oh, no, I don't think so.'

'But then you are not very experienced in recognising love when a man offers it to you, are you, *ma mie*?'

There seemed to be no answer to that, so she made none.

'We found Simone,' he continued eventually. 'Her car had skidded off the road and hit a wall.'

'Was she hurt?'

'No.' His lip curled. 'She is a great survivor, Simone. It took very little persuasion to get her to tell us what she had done with Philippe. She claimed it was a joke. I think she found it less amusing when she discovered that I was neither prepared to bring her back here nor drive her to the nearest garage.'

'You mean you abandoned her there?'

'Someone will discover her sooner or later,' he said almost idly. 'As I have said, she is a great survivor. Philippe, I think, is not. I have to thank you, *ma mie*, for your prompt action.'

'I don't need thanks,' she said hurriedly. 'I—I'm very fond of Philippe. I shall miss him.'

There was another loaded pause, then she said, very quickly, before her courage had a chance to fade, 'Blaise, I thought the worst of you without any justification, and although I know nothing can ever undo that, I want you to know I'm sorry. And there's another thing,' she added, afraid that he might interrupt. 'When we were—talking earlier, you said that I had hurt you by turning away from you on our wedding night because—I found you repulsive.' She took a deep breath. 'That—that just isn't true. I never have found you repulsive in any way.'

'Then why did you close your eyes and turn your head away when I was kissing you?' he asked.

'Because I didn't have anything on and I was shy,' she said baldly.

He raised an eyebrow. 'Give me my jacket,' he said, holding out his hand.

'That's mean,' she protested helplessly, holding it more tightly round her.

'Do you really find my looking at you so distasteful?'

'No,' she said honestly. 'Or at least I shouldn't if—if I could be sure why you were doing it. If it's to—teach me a lesson again, then it would be awful. And if it's because you're sending me away, and you'll probably never look at me again, that would be even worse.'

'And what if I tell you that to me—whether you're clinging to the back of a horse you can't ride, covered in soot, half-dressed or naked—you are all the beauty I have ever seen and that's why I want to look at you, and will do until I die? What then? Do you still imagine, *mon amour*, that I really intend to let you anywhere out of my sight?'

'Oh, Blaise!' Slow tears that she made no effort to check began to trickle down her face.

'I don't know what sort of life I am offering you,' he said. 'But it won't be easy, especially with Philippe feeling about me the way he does.'

'It will be better when he isn't an only child any more,' she said, smiling through her tears. 'Oh, Blaise, I love you.' She let the jacket slip to the floor and held out her arms to him. As he came to her, she lifted her face almost blindly to meet his kiss.

Eons later, lying with his head pillowed on her breasts, he murmured lazily, 'Did I hurt you?'

Andrea put up her hand, tenderly smoothing the hair back from his forehead. 'I didn't notice.'

'How shameless,' he said with a quiver of amusement in his voice.

She gave a sigh of utter contentment. 'We really ought to go and make sure that Philippe is all right.'

'Philippe is fine and already receiving more attention than he knows what to do with.' His arms tightened possessively round her. 'Don't be in too much of a hurry to leave our ivory tower, *ma mie*. The world can be a cruel place, as you have found.'

'But it can never touch us again,' she said dreamily.

'No.' Blaise lifted himself on to one elbow and looked down at her, his mouth twisted a little ruefully, but his eyes magically tender as he studied her, still flushed and glowing in the aftermath of their lovemaking. 'Don't expect too many miracles, *mon amour*. I don't want you to be hurt again.'

'How can I be hurt,' she said simply, 'with you to heal me?'

His lips were fierce on hers, but Andrea knew no qualms as she surrendered. Here, in this place of storms, she had found her haven at last.

Forthcoming Mills & Boon Romances

FLASH OF EMERALD *by Jane Arbor*
How could Hope possibly work for a man who was conceited enough to believe that all his secretaries fell in love with him?

SUNSET COUNTRY *by Dorothy Cork*
Saffi was relieved when Math Reyburn offered her the job of cook/travelling companion, but she had second thoughts when the sparks began to fly.

THE MASTER FIDDLER *by Janet Dailey*
Stranded with no transport and no money, Jacquie was grateful when Choya Barnett offered help – but then he named his price .....

CALL OF THE VELD *by Anne Hampson*
Carl van der Linden had no place for love in his life. – so had Sara considered what she was doing when she agreed to marry him?

NIGHT OF THE YELLOW MOON *by Flora Kidd*
Delia's marriage to Edmund had run into trouble, but was the Brazilian jungle the best place to sort things out?

NO SECOND PARTING *by Lilian Peake*
Logan Tate wanted a mother for his little daughter and who more suitable than Marianne, the girl he had walked out on eight years before!

SPINDRIFT *by Rebecca Stratton*
Bryony had always looked on her guardian, Dominic, as a rather forceful older brother, but then someone remarked on the 'irregularity' of their situation .....

LORD OF LA PAMPA *by Kay Thorpe*
Lian was in Ricardo's debt and it seemed that the only way she could repay him was by becoming his wife .....

GOLDEN APPLES *by Rose Elver*
Searching for her long-lost sister, Vere had problems enough – she just didn't need the added complication of falling in love!

SUNFLOWER SUMMER *by Sue Peters*
Nan loved country life and Doctor Keir Raven was too critical by half. But Nan was soon forced to re-assess the way she felt about him.

Mills & Boon Romances

– all that's pleasurable in Romantic Reading!

Available March 1978